THE
MULTIVERSE
1

NEW WORLDS

Jonathan Fetzner-Roell

BALBOA.PRESS

A DIVISION OF HAY HOUSE

Balboa Press books may be ordered through booksellers or by contacting:

Balboa Press
A Division of Hay House
1663 Liberty Drive
Bloomington, IN 47403
www.balboapress.com
844-682-1282

Because of the dynamic nature of the Internet, any web addresses or links contained in this book may have changed since publication and may no longer be valid. The views expressed in this work are solely those of the author and do not necessarily reflect the views of the publisher, and the publisher hereby disclaims any responsibility for them.

The author of this book does not dispense medical advice or prescribe the use of any technique as a form of treatment for physical, emotional, or medical problems without the advice of a physician, either directly or indirectly. The intent of the author is only to offer information of a general nature to help you in your quest for emotional and spiritual well-being. In the event you use any of the information in this book for yourself, which is your constitutional right, the author and the publisher assume no responsibility for your actions.

Any people depicted in stock imagery provided by Getty Images are models, and such images are being used for illustrative purposes only. Certain stock imagery © Getty Images.

Print information available on the last page.

ISBN: 979-8-7652-4203-2 (sc)
ISBN: 979-8-7652-4204-9 (e)

Balboa Press rev. date: 06/30/2023

With special thanks to coauthors Connor Harrity, Hunter Hopf, Emmett Ransdell, and Alan Navas-Brito

Contents

Part 3: Revived

Part 4: Amulets Arising

Acknowledgements

Hello. My name is Jonathan. I would like to thank Connor Harrity, Hunter Hoph, Emmett Ransdell, Damian Cain, AJ Waddell, Alan Navas-Brito, and more. Hopefully you will enjoy our book and the rest of the Multiverse series! We would all also like to thank you, reader, for buying and enjoying this book. So thank you to everyone!

Dedicated to Eli Mauck, a friend who can never be replaced.

Part 1

THE ELECTRIFYING WORLD

Chapter 1

EZRa

My name was Ezra Woods, and I was thirteen. I had twin brothers, Bryce and Matthew, who were seven and a half years old. I liked science as long as it was fun, like time machines.

"Hey, man, how is the experiment goin'?" asked Elijah.

"It's going great," I replied. You see, we had theorized that we could travel to the future.

"I just finished the right wing," I announced. "Getting close."

"Well, are we gonna test it or what?" asked Will curiously as he walked into the room.

"Test? Will, you know I still have to put on the antigenerator for it to be safe enough," I replied.

"Portal!" Bryce yelled as he ran in.

Just then, I was called home for dinner.

"Come on, Bryce. We gotta go."

On the walk home, I asked Bryce where Matthew was.

"He's at home. I got him hooked on a new video game." Bryce

was definitely more mature than Matthew, though he could be pretty loud. When we got home, my parents were waiting for us at the door.

"And where have you two been?" asked my mom.

"Out," I said, "with my friends."

"And why in the world was Bryce there?"

Bryce answered pretty fast, "Because I wanted to see their new invention." He gave me a mischievous smirk and left to go play video games.

I sat down at the dinner table.

"What are we having?"

"Don't change the subject," my mom said sternly.

My dad added, "You have to tell us where you went."

I said I wasn't hungry and went up to my room. As I lay in bed, I thought that maybe I could sneak out to start the left wing.

As I slept, I dreamed that I was in a room with my friends, and Elijah was talking about something. Suddenly, I couldn't see. It all turned black. I heard Corbin saying, "Ezra, wake up!" I also heard my mom saying "Ezra? Ezra, are you OK?" Lastly, I heard an unfamiliar voice. It said, "Ezra, welcome to the end." I woke up in a sweat. I shrugged fearful thoughts away and read for a while to take my mind off the dream. It had seemed so real but at the same time so dreamlike. "Just a dream," I said to myself. "It's not gonna hurt me." I opened the window to let in some fresh air and went to sleep.

The next morning, I woke to the sound of my brothers running and screaming.

It was Monday. Worst day of the week. I looked over at my clock—6:54 a.m. *Uh-oh.* Mom wants me awake before 6:50 a.m.

I got dressed and ready and went downstairs.

"Where have you been? It's past seven o' clock. Come and eat your breakfast," Mom said.

It didn't look like there would be any chance for me to work on the left wing before school.

I stared wide-eyed at the table. Soggy waffles. Yay.

"Your dad already left for work," Mom said. "Now hurry up and eat your breakfast."

A couple minutes later, I heard air brakes.

"There's the bus," Mom said. "Better get going."

The bus. A great way to add on to my fantastic day.

The bus was like it always was—loud and chaotic. The only thing different was that Will, Elijah, and Corbin weren't aboard. We soon arrived at school. As I entered my homeroom class, Mrs. Mannly, our homeroom teacher, said, "We have a lot of people absent today. We don't have Corbin, Elijah, Will, or Kylie."

Our homeroom class contains twenty-four kids. On a regular day, Elijah would be in front of me, but of course, he was absent.

I looked to my left side. Madison Holt was finishing our English homework. The bell went off.

"OK, class, time to turn your homework in." She had gone light on the homework.

The class all ran up toward the homework basket. When I finally got up there, Dwayne Parker, the teacher's pet and class bully, shoved me to the ground.

"Out o' my way, brainless."

I picked myself up, laid my paper in the basket, and went back to my desk.

I stared at my pages of work and the clock for the rest of class.

As the bell rang, Mrs. Mannly said, "OK, there's the bell. Have fun in PE."

I totally forgot that PE was after this. Sometimes it was good (kickball) and sometimes it was bad (push-ups).

As I arrived at the gym, it appeared that we were playing old-fashioned dodgeball. Toward the end of the game, I got nailed right in the eye. I was down for a solid two minutes.

The rest of the day was normal. Except for the end. When I was about to walk home, Dwayne and his gang dropped by. They picked me up and threw me onto the sidewalk. I landed with a loud screech. I ended up with a huge cut on my knee. I ran home and finally escaped them.

When I got home, I went straight to my room. A few minutes later, there was a knock on the door.

"It's Bryce." He walked into my room. "Holy cow!" he said. "What happened?"

"Bullies. It's fine."

Then I left to go work on the left wing.

But on my chair was a note that read:

> We tested the time portal. If you are reading this, we might be in a little bit of trouble.
> —Elijah

Uh-oh.

That's never good. I told them not to test it without the antigenerator! I experienced a weird feeling, though. I had no idea what called me to the portal, but the next thing I knew, I flew straight at the purple-blue screen. As the colors around me changed from purple to blue to violet, I thought, *I need to save my friends.*

Chapter 2

EZRa

As I flew through the portal, I realized that without the antigenerator, they couldn't have chosen the time they wanted to go to. They could be anywhere in the space-time continuum. That was the thing about the machine: you could pick where and what time with the antigenerator. I launched out of the other side of the portal.

"Elijah!" I shouted upon seeing my friend.

He lay on his back on the stone floor. Then I got my first look at my surroundings. The sky was a shade of harsh purple, and the roof was made of glass. The floor looked like stone at first sight, but upon further study, I saw that it was plated with diamonds, gold, and silver. Elijah looked as if he were glowing a bluish gray. Suddenly, a gray shockwave shot out from him. He launched up.

"How? What?" he asked.

It looked as if Elijah had no idea what was happening.

I helped Elijah to his feet, and we went to find the others. Locating them wasn't rocket science. Though, since I went in without the antigenerator, I got a cut on my left arm, not anything really bad though.

After we all got settled, we tried to figure out where we were. We were in a bright room. The door creaked open as we walked outside. And, man, did things look different. There were actual hoverboards cruising around. Had we really traveled into the future?

As we walked further, we realized that something felt odd. We saw the worried expressions on the people's faces. Then we saw it: the approaching black hole.

It was sweeping up everything in sight. We stood there paralyzed. Until it came for us. I didn't know why, but it seemed useless to run. As we were swarmed by the black hole, we saw something like a shock. It looked like something was fighting against the black hole.

And then it hit us. We were stuck. Colors started to fade, and soon our vision turned dark and we fainted.

While we were in the black hole, the aging process paused. There wasn't much to it. My friends and I were trapped in a black hole and came out one billion years later at the same age.

As we shot out of the black hole, we were all dazed by the glimpse of daylight. But the glimpse was short. When we hit the ground, we couldn't see anything.

I opened my eyes and realized I was in a hospital. I was told by some sort of different species that I was very lucky to be alive.

I looked at my hand and saw a cut on my right palm. It was squiggly, and anybody could make out its lightning bolt shape.

I was so relieved when Corbin woke up.

"What happened?" he asked.

"Er … black hole incident."

"Oh."

"It looks like we've traveled to a different … planet?" I said.

"You think?" he said as he looked at the alien that entered the room.

"You will be undertaking medical care," the alien said.

"What's that?" I asked.

"We're just gonna keep you here for a few days," the doctor said.

"Yay," Corbin mumbled loud enough for me and the doctor to hear.

"It won't be all that bad," Doc said. "It's only for a couple of days. Usually, it would be a lifetime, but your bodies stopped the aging process, which also stopped how old your lungs got. Your lungs and bones are still at the average age of a thirteen-year-old."

"I was hoping for two hours, not a few days." Corbin mumbled again, this time making sure Doc couldn't hear him.

With that, Doc left the room.

"Ugh, I'm gonna hate this," Corbin said. "This is my fault, Ezra. I had the idea of testing the time machine. I'm sorry."

I thought about it for a minute. "Don't be sorry. We're on another planet. We solved one of science's biggest mysteries. Time travel. Albert Einstein tried to make it, but he couldn't figure it out. But we could, and we're only thirteen. Well, maybe like 1,000,000,013."

He chuckled a little bit and said, "Well, I guess falling into a black hole and staying there for one billion years and getting medical care from aliens is worth solving a scientific mystery."

Just then, Will woke up. Elijah woke up shortly after that. There was a TV in the room, a really advanced one. It didn't even have a remote. We turned it on by pressing the button on our table. The news blasted on.

"Breaking news: the DM continues preparing for war against us while we still remain with almost absolutely nothing to fight with," said the news analyst.

"What's the DM?" asked Will.

"Looks like that," I reply, pointing to the different universe on the screen. Just then, bright blue lightning blasted out of the cut on my hand. It shot straight at what I pointed to on the screen. The TV sparked and turned black.

I looked around the room. On everyone's face I saw excitement but also fear. Was it true? Did I have superpowers? I knew they were thinking about two things: One, I now had superpowers. And two, this place wasn't another planet; it was another universe.

Chapter 3

EZRA

I was worried what Doc would say about the TV. Surprisingly, he acted normally.

"Yes, we thought that would happen," he said.

"You mean you expected Ezra to explode a TV by shooting lightning out of his hand?"

"Of course not," Doc said. "We expected you guys to have powers. If Ezra has them, you guys must too."

"Epic!" yelled Will

"Awesome!" yelled Corbin

"Amazing!" yelled Elijah

I was still standing there, shocked.

Slowly and loudly, my friends start cheering.

"I wonder what my powers will be," Corbin thinks aloud.

But then the noise faded out, and it became hard to see. I realized something. One billion years later. Mom, Dad, Bryce, Matthew were gone. Everyone except Corbin, Elijah, and Will. There was no way someone I used to know was living one billion years later. How had I not figured this out earlier? My bruises didn't hurt anymore. All the pain had moved to my heart.

"What's wrong?" Will asked.

"Nothing," I said. I didn't want to spread the news to my friends. But he read my mind.

"I know," he said. "They're gone. But we can get past it. Keep our minds off it."

"We can try," I said, but in my mind, I knew we can't.

I knew it would haunt me for the rest of my life. None of my family was with me anymore. I'd just traveled one billion years into the future, and it all happened so fast. Nobody acted like it was a big deal. We'd just found life on other planets in like two seconds, while astronauts had been trying for years. It was kind of weird living in a world populated with aliens. I was very surprised on the inside, but I didn't want to hurt the aliens' feelings. It really put my mind into high gear. How would we get out of here, or were we going to get out of here? Also, what about the food? Was it like stuff from Earth, or some outer space gunk that we had never heard of before. Either way, I hoped it wasn't disgusting.

Apparently Will had been thinking the same thing because he asked me if I had seen the food. I replied, "No. I just hope it actually tastes like food."

Will said, "I have! The only food here is pizza and ice cream."

While that sounded good at the time, after two weeks of it, I felt like never eating pizza again. The only drinks were lemonade and—well, I never got tired of it—root beer. Yes!

Chapter 4

EZRA

The next two weeks of my life were as boring as ever. I could sense it in my friends too. I really wanted to test me and my friends' powers to see what they had. We mostly wanted to be ready for the attack from the DM.

I also really wanted to figure out what day it was, but as I suspected, the days were different here:

Monday = Singaday
Tuesday = Doubleday
Wednesday = Triday
Thursday = Quaday
Friday = Quinday
Saturday =Hexaday
Sunday = Sepday

It took time, but I finally realized that my birthday was in three weeks, on July 19. That meant today was June 29.

And just like that, we were out of medical care.

"It really wasn't that bad," said Corbin. "Pizza and ice cream the whole time."

"I'm getting kinda bored of pizza and ice cream," said Elijah.

"Maybe we can invent something else," Will said, just now coming into the conversation.

"We can focus on that later," I said. "For now we have to prepare."

"And we gotta go fast," agreed Elijah. "We have no idea when the DM will strike."

"Fast but carefully," I reply.

The next day was all about prep. We went to the gym, and it was pretty big. Then I saw something I never thought I would see again.

There was a girl. A human girl. The only humans I thought I'd probably see for the rest of my life were my friends. She looked to be about my age. The girl was doing something in the corner of the gym that I couldn't quite see. The rest of my team was shocked too. How would another human make it here?

We were all stunned, except Elijah. He was most focused on his "Ooooooooohs" just because I saw a human girl! I would get him later. Right now, we had a bigger problem: the DM.

As we walked to the target practice room, we got some weird looks. Some of the aliens thought we were awesome and wanted our human autographs, but others thought we didn't belong here. We definitely stood out. But they were right. We didn't belong here.

"I wonder how long this will take," Will said as we entered the room.

"Man, it's hot in here," said Corbin. "Can we turn the temperature down?"

"Sure," I said. I found the thermostat and turned it down a notch.

After about an hour, we had it figured out: Corbin had fire,

Elijah had water, Will had light, and I had all my friends' powers combined, plus lightning.

Before we left, I asked someone what the DM was. I made sure it was someone who liked us. They told us that the DM stood for "Dark Multiverse," which meant there were good and evil multiverse dimensions.

As we left, we saw a darkened figure approaching us. He stopped and stared at us. Then he shot a blue beam right at us. I blocked the attempt with my force field. Corbin took a shot, but the man deflected it. Then the man held his hand out, and a beam darted at Corbin, who was defenseless. The blue beam blasted him, and he fell to the ground. Elijah had snuck behind the figure for some reason.

"Hey!" Elijah yelled. "What's yo problem?"

"The problem?" the man answered. "The problem is this universe."

I had no problem guessing who this was. The Dark Multiverse. I knew that they would strike, but I had never thought it would happen this fast. Just then, I realized something I had never thought would happen. My friends and I were the most powerful people in our universe. There was no way our universe could win this war without us. We had no choice but to fight.

Chapter 5

EZRA

The creepy man disappeared. He antigenerated, meaning he, like, melted into the ground and teleported. We ran over to Corbin.

I checked him over and asked, "Are you OK, dude?"

"Hurts. But I'm good."

"We'll need you."

"Thanks, man."

"Speaking of," I said. "We have to find the DM's base."

"Dude," Elijah said. "It's in the Dark Multiverse. Duh."

"It's actually not," said Corbin. "There is an antigenerate range. You can't antigenerate from one dimension or universe to another. The range is about nine hundred miles. But the antigenerator has no limit. Though sometimes you can break the barrier. It's usually some kind of emotion."

Corbin was definitely the brainiest in our group. If he was sad or hurt and we asked him a challenging question, he would instantly try to solve it and would forget what he was upset about. No kidding.

"So you're saying their base is within nine hundred miles of here?" Will asked.

"Yup."

"Great."

We went back to the gym the next day. We knew the DM would strike when they wanted to. And they did. While I was practicing my target aiming, the ceiling split apart and flames tore down the building. I was knocked out. When I woke up, Corbin, Will, Elijah, and the girl were staring at me. I realized there was something familiar about her. It was Madison Holt! The girl from my class! Madi had some sort of first aid kit and was healing a burn on my hand.

When she was done, I asked, "How do you know how to do that?

"My mom used to be a nurse. I've picked up a few things."

"We're gonna need a medical assistant in this war. I'm expecting way worse than a couple of grenades," Elijah said. "You can, er ... join us? I mean, we are in the same class," he added like a wimp.

"You want me? A team would be great."

"So what do you say?" I asked.

"I'd say it would be a better way to survive. I'll take you up on your offer. Yes," she said.

A short time later, we arrived at our "hut" (which was a fifteen-foot-tall fort). The guys stayed outside, while Madi and I went inside to talk.

"Let's start simple," I said. "We know your name, of course, but what are your powers?"

"*Um*, let's see ..." she said, looking down. "Mind control, force field, antigenerate, invisibility. Stuff like that."

"OK, do you know anyone else here?"

"Nope. I've been running the streets for a while."

"Last question: how did you get here?"

"I was born with my powers. My dad was falsely accused of

robbery and was arrested, and my mom died of cancer. Back then I was only five. I didn't know how to control my powers. I got so mad when I heard about my parents, I accidentally antigenerated here. I know the antigenerate limit, but I guess it takes great emotion to get past the barrier."

An awkward silence fell between us.

"Glad, you're on our team."

"Same here."

"We have to be ready for the DM," I said as I took a bite of the food my friends made. *"Ahh!* Gross!"

Madi chuckled, and I smiled.

"Come on, guys," I called to my friends, who were still outside. "We're going to the city."

Chapter 6

EZRA

We were walking along the sidewalk when Corbin looked into the air. A plane was flying low, and soon it landed on a cement road. I saw a man step out and stare at us. He was far away, but I could still see his hand glowing with lightning sparking around it.

"*Uh-oh*," said Madison. "Hold on!"

I felt myself get pulled into something, and immediately, we all appeared in our hideout. We had antigenerated. The hideout wasn't big.

"Hey. Uh, I'm gonna go back and check out the plane. That's gotta be someone from the Dark Multiverse. It may take a while if it gets bad, so if I'm not back by dark, just know I'll stay in a hotel. Hotels are free here," Madi said.

"All right," I replied. "Be careful."

She antigenerated away. I wanted to ask her why we all couldn't get a hotel instead of using the hideout since hotels were free. But that was a question for another day. I lay on the ground, closed my eyes, and fell asleep.

I woke up to Corbin tugging on me.

"Come on," he said. "We have to check on Madi."

"All right," I said wearily.

I got up and walked outside with Corbin. When we walked a little farther, we found something that caught us off guard. The plane from yesterday had been torn into pieces, and there was fire everywhere. It turned out it wasn't even a plane; it was just a flying automobile. I looked up and saw a massive skyscraper with the words "Skitt Hotels" on it. We ran inside.

"Hi. Do you have someone here named Madison Holt?" I asked.

"*Um* … let's see here," the alien said. "Madison Holt checked out with a man named Dr. Virgil Phoenix." Then the same thing that happened when I realized the things about my parents happened to me again. The only thing different was the voice inside my head: "We have her. Come find us if you want to save her. Don't die," it said.

Corbin and I ran out the door as fast as we could and all the way to the hideout.

"They have Madi."

We got ready faster than the speed of light. I couldn't believe the Dark Multiverse had her. We ran out of the base. Lightning sparked from my fingers at every angle. Elijah had placed a tracking device in the cloak of the man from the gym. Surprisingly, their base wasn't that far away. But it was one of the biggest things I'd ever seen.

We beat up four guards and stole their suits.

"These are way too big," Elijah complained.

"We'll have to wear them. That's all we have," I replied.

We opened the doors. Standing there was the "ruler" of the Dark Multiverse. Dr. Virgil Phoenix. He was surprisingly human.

"We've been expecting you," Dr. Phoenix said.

He shot us with a bolt of lightning, and we were dazed. He ordered his guards to throw us into cells. Right before they put us in there, they stuck needles into our arms and injected us with something that took our powers away for twenty-four hours. We were stuck here. We were the prisoners of the universe.

My cell was next to Elijah and Madison. Across from me was Will's cell. Diagonally was Corbin's.

"Come on," said a guard as he opened my jail cell. "We're taking you to the questioning room."

I walked out and saw two guards, both wearing white suits with white armor and gray undershirts. Their masks were white and had blue visors. One of the men had a large gun in his hand. The other was cuffing me. I looked at their utility belts. They each had different colored blasters with blue and red chemicals swirling around in their barrels. Once the guard finished restraining me, he held my arm and walked us down the hall while the other stood behind me, prepared for anything. We saw the door of the questioning room. The guard opened it for me, and I walked in. A chair stood in the middle of the room, and in the corners were guards wearing the same uniforms as the ones bringing me in, except theirs were black. Dr. Phoenix stood behind the chair. I sat down in it, and Dr. Phoenix walked closer.

"Let's start simple," he said. "What do you know?"

"Nothing. I know nothing."

He sighed. "We thought you'd say that. But let's put it this way. If you don't tell us, then you, your friends, and everyone in your universe will die."

"We'd still die if I give you information," I said.

He paused. "Guards."

"I'm not scared of you," I said.

He laughed. "You will be," he said, still staring at me.

All the guards left the room. He snapped his fingers, and a screen appeared on the wall in front of me with a picture of Earth on it. "You see that?

"Yeah."

"I'll blow it up," he said. "With your siblings on it."

"My siblings are dead."

He raised his eyebrows in surprise. "They're not dead, Ezra." He spoke softly but sternly. "Bryce and Matthew are still alive."

"You're lying," I said.

"You may believe that, but if they are, then Earth will come to an end. So tell me. Or else you take the risk of your siblings dying."

"They're not alive."

"If you say so," he said and nodded toward the camera.

I looked at the screen, and a blast shot toward Earth. It hit, and the world exploded into a ball of white fire. Soon, the fire disappeared and the planet we all knew was gone.

"No!" I screamed.

"Now give me what I want, or I'll blow up your universe."

Just then I heard screaming coming from outside. The door blasted open, and a person in a red suit of armor was standing there pointing his blaster at Dr. Phoenix. The blaster had a barrel with blue chemicals in it.

"Let him go," the person said.

"No."

"You have two options," the person responded. "I shoot you and I release him, or you release him and I let you go." He talked with a slanglike accent.

"All right then, take him," Dr. Phoenix said.

The person in red shot a laser at my chair, and the ropes around my arms dissolved. I ran up and darted down the hallway without even saying anything to the man who saved me. I stopped at Madi's door and lit the lock into a flame. The door creaked open, and Madi stepped out.

"Thank you so much!" she said and hugged me. I ran over to Elijah's cell and blew it open too. I went to the cell of Corbin, who lay on his bed.

"What are you doing?" he whisper-yelled at me.

"Getting you out of here," I replied.

Then I went to Will's cell and broke him out too.

"Oh, thank God," he said.

We looked forward and saw a door. We rushed to it and blew it open.

"Ohhhh!" I screamed. The door was on the side of the building, and my momentum carried me off the edge.

"I got you!" Will yelled. He grabbed my hand in the nick of time. I was hanging by one hand four stories up. I pressed my feet against the wall and pulled myself back through the door.

"Thank you," I said.

Just then, a thin line shot across from our building to the next. I looked up to the roof, and standing there was the man in red. He saluted, dropped his grappling hook launcher, and flew off with his jet pack. He was saving us again.

"I don't like this," Corbin said. "It's like traveling from building to building on a clothesline!"

I looked behind us and heard guards running down the hallway. "We don't have much of a choice," I told him.

I jumped as far as I could and wrapped my hands around the line. I had a good grip, and I wanted it to stay that way. I moved one arm in front of the other.

This isn't so scary, I thought to myself, *just like monkey bars.* Once I reached the end of the line, I gathered all my momentum and flung myself onto the balcony. Next was Will, who came over with ease. Then Madi, who closed her eyes the entire time. And then came Corbin. He gripped his hands around the rope and swung over the alley below. He screamed but gathered his strength shortly after. He moved his trembling hands one in front of the other and eventually got to the other side.

"Good job!" I assured him.

We blew open the door as gazes from across the alley fell upon us. We didn't care. We ran down the stairs and into the road. After all that, my friends and I were finally free.

Chapter 7

EZRa

The next day, I saw a newspaper headline: "The DM disappears to different parts of the planet in search of the 'Powered Kids.'" That was weird. The powered kids.

Minutes later, I heard a rustling coming from the leaves outside our hut. I opened the door.

"We need you," said the woman outside. "Now. We will explain in the van. Trust us."

We decided to trust them, but even if they were bad, we still had our powers. So we went with them.

"You said you would explain this. So explain," Corbin said impatiently when we were all in the van.

"Yes," the woman said. "We are taking you to a hiding compound."

"Hiding?" Elijah screamed. "We don't need to hide! We need to fight!"

"You can fight when they attack the compound."

"Well then, it's not safe if they're attacking it."

"Fine. Where are we going?"

"An open country land in Zykele."

"What the heck is that?"

"A safe place."

It got boring really fast in the van. Until Madi noticed a car behind us.

"Wow. Look at that car!" Madi said. "Protected steel wheels, a double plated windshield, and a top antenna. That's either a super fancy police car or they're following us."

"Really?"

"Yeah."

Just then, an explosion hit right under the car.

"Go!" I screamed.

And the chase was on.

The driver of the vehicle behind us also picked up speed. I saw the man in the passenger seat roll down his window and shoot a laser beam at the back windshield. The bright red laser blasted a hole through it. Then they shot a laser at the wheel. The van went crazy and fell off a bridge and into the water.

The long drop was horrible. I watched the scene go down. Literally. And the car went underwater, and soon the inside was completely flooded. We were all stuck until Madi exploded the car with a force field. We were suddenly out in open water. And then I thought of the worst thing I could think at the time: *Corbin can't swim.*

I saw him struggling as he sank. I wanted to help him, but I couldn't. I had just a few seconds of air left. I saw the desperation in his eyes. I knew what I should do. It was the thought that counted.

I swam as fast as I could toward him and grabbed his hand. But then I ran out of air. *This is how people die*, I thought. Then I saw the light. Not the light to heaven but the light of electricity. Water grabbed us, and we shot straight up. I smiled. It was Elijah. He was helping us.

As Corbin and I came to the surface, we gasped for air.

"Where's Will and Madi?" I asked.

"Over here," Will screeched. *Uh-oh.*

I swam over to the voice. Part of the van had Will and Madi pinned against the rocks. The waves went toward them, which did not help. I went in for a closer look. It was pressed against Will's chest.

As we pushed the large piece of the van away, Will went under. He popped back up shortly after, though.

"Where's the woman?" Corbin asked.

"I don't know," Will replied.

"How are we gonna get outta here?"

"I don't know."

"So we're stuck?

"That's what it seems like."

"Great."

"Wait," Madi said. "I forgot to tell you about one of my other powers. Portal control."

"Well, that'll come in handy right about now."

So Madi took us back up onto the bridge. But the car that shot our wheels was still there, so Corbin blasted the truck with fire and it fell into the water.

"Time to give DM a taste of its own medicine."

Chapter 8

EZRa

Even though we never found the woman, we later heard that she was all right. We still made it to the compound because when she had told us that the compound was in Zykele, Corbin had used his new upgraded watch to bring up a map so we could walk there.

The compound was amazing. It had a gym, a lounge, an indoor-outdoor pool, and a hot tub.

It wasn't long before we heard the DM's next attack. The battle area was only two miles away. We heard a loud explosion. We ran up the hill and saw a large hole in the ground; it was about the size of a large meteorite. We saw people walking away from the hole with their hands up. Cars were parked around it. They were taking random citizens as prisoners! As we helplessly walked back to the compound, I decided to go to the pool.

I sat on the edge with my feet dipping into the water. I thought about what had happened. Nothing could describe my feelings for the Dark Multiverse.

After a while, Elijah and Will walked in. We talked for a while until Will said, "OK, I gotta go. They made us dinner. Some new food."

When Will left, Elijah started talking: "I think I can change it."

"Change it?" I asked. "You can't change what Phoenix is doing."

"I can."

I sigh. "What do you have in mind?"

"Well, if we use the time machine to go back in time, we can eliminate Phoenix's ancestors, making a chain reaction to where he wasn't even born."

"How would we travel to the past without the time machine?"

"Well, if we went back to the spot we first came into, maybe there would be something we could use."

"We can try."

Elijah was kind of disappointed that I wasn't excited. I was ... but I wasn't in the mood to show it.

As Elijah went to the door to leave, I said, "I mean, how bad can they get?"

"I'm not sure, but I know it's not over," he responded.

Part 2

FIGHT FOR LIFE

Chapter 9

EZRA

Ever since Dr. Phoenix took prisoners, we had heard absolutely nothing about any DM movements. That got on my nerves because we wanted our chance at redemption.

The crew and I found the road we had originally come here from. As we neared the exact spot, we were stunned by what we saw: a pair of green glowing eyes. Even weirder, they were swirling like smoke, and then the eyes changed to yellow.

"Who are you?" Will yelled at the eyes.

And then everything turned black again.

We woke up dizzy, with a bunch of mostly orange but some purple and red colors swirling around us.

"Foolish. You all are. Your desire to be like some superhero with your powers is pathetic," a voice echoed throughout the tube-shaped area in which we found ourselves confined.

"Let us out!" I screamed.

"You have two choices. We will let you out lifeless or ... we will let you out alive if you join us."

"What? But aliens have the same amount of power that we do. And they are probably way smarter than humans."

"Yes, I've learned that humans think aliens are the smartest things ever. But there are few aliens left that are equal to human intelligence."

This was by far the biggest decision of my life. Because ... it could end it.

In a comic book, the superhero would definitely sacrifice himself, but it felt weird asking someone to do that. What would our answer be? We would have to work with them.

"Fine, we'll work with you."

"Good."

The colors went away, and we were standing in front of the most horrible place in history. The DM's castle.

"Go in," he said.

"*Um* ... a moment with my friends?" Madison said.

He sighed. "Fine. You have thirty seconds."

"I can antigenerate us away from this place so we won't have to work with them. But I need to know where to go."

I almost suggested the compound, but unfortunately, we had just realized that the Dark Multiverse had invaded it.

"What about the lair thing I built?"

"That's probably the only option we have."

"Then it's settled."

As we walked toward Dr. Phoenix very casually, we turned into smoke and went straight to the hideout.

Chapter 10

EZRA

"OK, I got the stuff you needed," Madi said as she walked into the hideout. "Invisibility is a really good talent to have when you're desperately gathering stuff to survive. I got food, water, a book for Corbin, a target for Will, a book on water for Elijah, and a basketball for Ezra."

"And for yourself?" I asked.

"Some superenergized candy." She shrugged. "Tastes good."

I looked at my phone. I wondered if I texted my mom's phone it actually send. Or would it say, "Message failed to send"?

I tried.

I sent a number one to her phone. To my surprise, under the message it said, "Delivered." That was cool and creepy at the same time!

That night, I had set my phone down to go to sleep when suddenly it dinged and the screen flashed on. It read, "Message: Mom Message."

Had my mom's text just sent me something? I grabbed my phone, entered my passcode, and went straight to the text app. The texter had written, "Hello." I quickly texted back. Our conversation read:

Me: 1
Mom: Hello
Me: Who is this?
Mom: Some scary guy
Me: Seriously, what is going on?
Mom: Fine. It's Matthew and Bryce
Me: What the heck!!!!!
Me: I need proof
Me: What color hair does Matthew have?
Mom: Easy, blond
Me: Holy cow!!
(You spelled blonde wrong)Me: How are you guys alive?
Mom: We snuck in the time portal and got sucked up by the black hole but didn't go to a different universe
Me: So where are you?
Mom: Earth, duh
Me: Phoenix said you up he blew you up
Mom: Then that guy is a liar. P.S. Who is he?!
Me: Long story, the bad guy
Me: I'm coming for you guys tomorrow
Mom: Yeah, come fast. We need your help

I couldn't believe they were alive. But for now, I just needed some rest.

I woke up and told my friends about my siblings. We went outside to plan how we'd get there. We had no ideas. We couldn't fly there. We had nothing. That's when I got mad.

"I promised I'd come for them!" I yelled. "I can't leave them now that I know they are alive!"

Anger got the best of me. I sat on the ground. Just then, I turned to smoke and antigenerated. I broke the range. I didn't know I could antigenerate! Suddenly, I was on Earth. It was completely gray. Smoke was everywhere, and all around me soldiers searched for signs of life. What had happened to this world where I used to live?

"*Oww*," I heard a quiet screech as I looked under the huge piece of metal. Hiding there were Bryce and Matthew.

"P-p-please don't hurt us," Bryce said worriedly.

"It's Ezra, you dummy," Matthew said.

"Ezra … is that you?" Bryce asked timidly.

I felt so relieved at that moment. They were alive. I could not wait any longer to tell my friends. Friends. I wondered if I could ever get back to them. I didn't know the sacrifice I was making.

Chapter 11

ezra

I started to wonder if Matthew and Bryce had powers, because they did everything we had done. Went to the future. Got sucked up by a black hole. They just didn't end up in a different universe, or galaxy, or planet, for that matter.

I realized that if we went back home, I could get the time machine and go back to my friends. I looked at our surroundings. I knew Bryce and Matthew wouldn't have gone far from home. But I couldn't really tell because there was nothing. My watch told me, though. I was right. It was only a block away. When I entered the pitch-black room, the time machine was glowing. I needed to find the antigenerator so I could choose where we went.

It took some looking around, but I finally located it. I placed the antigenerator on the time portal, and my brothers and I went back to my friends.

We appeared in the hideout. My friends were packing.

"Madi," I said. "This is Bryce and Matthew. Bryce, Matthew," I said as I pointed at Madi, "this is Madison."

"Hello."

"Hi."

"Why are you guys packing?" I asked.

"Some guy offered to let us to stay with him. He promised not to tell people where we are."

As we entered the man's house, I realized he was rich. Really rich. His pool was even fancy. He told us to make ourselves at home. The first thing we did was use the pool. When I jumped into the water, I accidentally surged. Fortunately, I was the first one in, so no one got shocked. Unfortunately, as my electricity hit the water, it burned down my whole body. It left a huge cutlike burn from just over my heart all the way down to my stomach. Flames and a burning sensation emanated from around the wound.

"*Ahh!*" I screamed as loud as I could. "Help!"

I was starting to drown. Smoke billowed off my chest. The shape of a lightning bolt was burned into my blue shirt. Everyone started moving at once. Will jumped in to help me, Elijah ran to get towels, Corbin moved a lounge chair toward side of the pool, and Madi hurried inside for her phone and her first aid kit.

Will pulled me out of the water and onto the chair. Elijah laid the towel over me, and Madi ran out with the kit.

"Should I contact the ER?" Corbin asked.

"They won't get here in time. ER is going to be the last chance and only if we have to. You can look up how to heal a wound like this, though," Madi said.

"Please. Please help me," I groaned.

"I'm going as fast as I can," Will said.

"It, it hurts," I said. "*Ahh!*" I screamed as water soaked into the cut. "It stings!"

"What are we gonna do?" Elijah asked. "We can't shock him 'cuz he'll absorb it."

"I'm sorry," I said weakly. I couldn't take it anymore. I passed out.

"Noooo!" Corbin screamed. "Come on, buddy. Don't die on us." Tears filled Corbin's eyes. "Come on, come on. Stay with me."

Just then, Will took me back into the water. He hoped it would help the burn. *Just don't surge*, he thought.

It didn't work. He brought me back up to the chair.

"I did as much as I could," Madi said.

Corbin laid his head to my heart. "It's not beating."

Just then, Matthew and Bryce came bursting into the pool room.

"Ezra!" they both screamed. "Nooo!"

Everyone just stood there, helplessly.

Corbin stared at me, teary-eyed, Elijah prayed, Madi stood with her jaw hanging open, Will closed his eyes as hard as he could, and Matthew and Bryce kneeled on the ground, hanging their heads.

"He-I-he's gone," Corbin said sadly.

Chapter 12

CORBIN

My full name was Corbin Kennly. This was my friend Ezra's story, but I took over because he was ... *um* ... gone.

A few weeks after Ezra's death, I found out the twins' powers. Bryce had a connection through eternity, and Matthew had like, uh ... flowing electricity ... kind of. One day, I found Bryce sitting in the corner of an empty room in the rich man's house. (His name was Vadg.)

"What's going on?" I asked.

"I-w-I—There's something inside of me. I can feel it. It's ... cold."

This ... was creepy.

That night as I went to sleep, I heard Bryce whine. He groaned and flopped on his pillow. I wanted to help him, but it wasn't like I knew how.

I looked into his room.

"Please help me," he begged, lying helplessly on his bed.

The next day, we were all talking about our siblings when Matthew spoke up.

"When me and Bryce were on Earth, we saw Abi and Brinx. Some DM guard was taking them away. They said they were taking them to the Phoenix Force Tower."

Abi, or Abigail, was my sister. She was the same age as me, but we were not twins. She was just a little bit younger than me. Brinx was Will's twelve-year-old cousin.

"The Phoenix Force Tower?" Will asked.

"My guess is that it's the Dark Multiverse HQ."

"Do you know where that is?"

"No idea."

"Wait. I think I heard of a building downtown in Zykele, but I was gonna wait and tell you guys once I had more information on it," Madi said.

"Then we're going downtown," I said immediately.

Chapter 13

CORBIN

As we walked the streets of downtown, we noticed it looked ... different. Strange vehicles were driving everywhere. Matthew would have loved this, but he and Bryce had stayed at the base.

Eventually, we found the Phoenix Force Tower. We had just walked through the gated entrance when suddenly the guards pointed their laser blasters at us.

"You need to show us your ID card!" one guard demanded.

"Fine," Elijah said as he pulled out his fake ID card. He had faked his name and age. "Here it is." He handed the card to the guard.

"Your name is Aardy Punitia?"

"Yup."

When the guard looked back down at the card, Elijah punched him hard in the face.

"Hey!" one of the other guards yelled. "Fire! Fire!"

But Madi quickly flicked her fingers, and a force field shot out toward the guards, knocking them down.

As we continued toward the tower, we saw a sign by the door. It warned us that there were virus vaccines in testing and said if we got sick, it was not their fault. It was like the waivers you had to sign in jump parks.

We walked into the lobby and hoped Dr. Phoenix wouldn't see us. We found the nicest-looking person and asked where our siblings were.

"Why do you need them?" the man asked me.

"I … uh … Phoenix wants them. He sent me to get them!"

The man was suspicious, but he told us that Brinx was in room 4 and Abi was in room 15. Of course, I rescued Abi and Will rescued Brinx.

Will busted open the door with a laser and found Brinx lying on his bed.

The alarm went off.

"Come on, Brinx! We're saving you! Let's go!"

"Uhhh … I—" Brinx groaned.

Will grabbed Brinx's arm and pulled him out of the cell.

"Come on. We gotta go."

"I can't—"

Will let go of Brinx's arm, and he fell straight to the ground.

"Brinx!"

"I c-c-can't w-walk. I-I-I have the v-virus."

Will was stunned. He grabbed Brinx and gave him to Madi.

"Take care of Brinx. He has the virus. Get everyone except Phoenix Force out of the building."

"OK, but what are you gonna do?"

"Business."

Chapter 14

CORBIN

Will broke into the virus lab. The doctors screamed at him,

"Young man, you're not allowed in here."

"The virus will escape!"

Will walked into the lab. He pulled out some sort of gun from his belt and shot it at his hand. Out came a ball full of UD (ultradynamite).

"You better not turn that on. None of us deserve to go that way."

"You work for Phoenix," Will said.

"But you wouldn't set it off with yourself in the building ... would you?"

"Yes, I would." He set the bomb for thirty seconds and walked out of the room.

Please be out of the building, he thought about his friends and brother. *Please.*

The building exploded with a loud *bang*.

"I think Will was still in it," Elijah said when we were all outside. "But other than that, the building was completely empty."

Through the fire and smoke, we caught sight of Will standing on the ground.

Just then, the emergency vehicles came. We lifted Brinx into an ambulance. They said we could all ride in the back.

We were on our way to the hospital, when I got a call from Matthew.

"Bryce just fell to the ground and he's not moving! We need help ... Hurry!"

We were just about a mile out from the hideout on the way to the hospital. I told the driver to drop me and Elijah off at the house and to call another emergency vehicle there. We ran up to the house and swung open the door. Bryce lay on the ground, out cold.

"What was going on?" I asked.

"Something was like ... hitting him ... He was flinching."

"Where's Vadg?" I asked.

"He left."

"He left you by yourselves?"

"Yup."

Just then, the emergency vehicle arrived. We loaded Bryce into the back and rode alongside him. At the hospital, the doctors told us that Bryce would probably be fine, but Brinx was fifty-fifty. We went into Brinx's room and looked at the heart monitor. It was doing good ... at least we thought it was. Until it turned into a straight line.

We turned around to call the doctors, and Madi ran toward Brinx. It would be crazy if Brinx died the day before Ezra's birthday. As we turned around, there stood Dr. Phoenix, Colvin Phoenix, and most sadly of all, Julian Phoenix. Colvin was thirteen. Julian was twelve; he was the evilest of the Phoenix kids.

"What do you want?" I asked.

"To capture you. Isn't that obvious?" Julian said with a smirk. "Hey!" he yelled at Madi. "Get away from him!"

Just then the lights flickered and turned off, plunging the room into pitch-black darkness.

That was right. Colvin didn't have fire or laser but rather a mix, which gave him access to lights. Julian had superspeed and ice powers.

Colvin's eyes turned red in the darkness. Suddenly, I flew back against the wall. I felt ice trap me against it.

"Help!" I yelled.

Then the ice turned into boiling water when Colvin blasted it.

"*Ahh!*" I fell to the ground.

Suddenly the lights flickered on. Except the Phoenix Force was gone.

"We must find them. They're more powerful than ever."

Chapter 15

CORBIN

We ran toward Brinx. The heart monitor was up again. What had happened? As the monitor went back to normal, Brinx woke up.

"I couldn't breathe. What happened?" Brinx said.

"Phoenix," I mumbled. "We're going to need to split up if we want to find him. Me, Elijah, Bryce, and Matthew will search east. Madi, Will, and Abi will search west. Brinx, stay here."

For about an hour we searched for the Phoenix Force. No luck. The doctors said it was a miracle that Brinx would be released so quickly.

As we were about to enter our headquarters, we saw a sign on the door.

Party time!
This is an invitation to come to our amazing
party for Quin-Seppa Day. Our day of freedom

against Banter's Legacy Legion! Come to the
building on 116 Street.

This was perfect. We could look around to see if there were any
clues.

The next day was a sad day. It was Ezra's birthday. Though the
day after that was different. The party was held at the top of the
building, which had a pool. I looked at it in disgust. I sat down and
suddenly realized how our siblings had gotten here. Bryce had said
something about him getting all our siblings together to try and find
us when our parents had been looking with search parties. They had
called all our classmates. Brinx must have jumped into the portal
when Bryce was on the phone with Madison. When you jumped
into a portal, it sent out an electric surge for half a mile. If you were
inside the half a mile radius, you would teleport too. That meant the
siblings had gone through the portal too. But the phone lines mixed
with the portal lines and affected Madi. But Ezra had neighbors.
That meant anyone inside the half mile radius was in this universe
too. But the weird thing was that Ezra had a billionaire neighbor.
That had to be Dr. Phoenix!

Will took Brinx to the pool house.

"What happened to you, man? It looks like they treated you the
worst," Will asked.

"Yeah. They didn't like how I stood up for every torture they
did on us."

"Your hair even looks different. It used to be spiked and faded
with that green stroke, but now it's just messy."

"I know. I'm supposed to get a haircut tomorrow."

There was a rocketlike noise outside.

"What was that?" Will asked.

"I don't know. Let's check it out."

They walked out of the pool house. A huge missile was about to
smash into the top of the building. Suddenly, a bright blue shield of
electricity covered the building. I saw a person on the diving board

create it. The person was hard to see as the light shot past him. He appeared to be dark. After about thirty seconds, the missile dissolved after trying to work its way through the shield. The person pulled it down, was shocked by lightning, and disappeared. Though, for a brief second, I was sure I saw that he was wearing a jersey with the word "Woods" on the back—Ezra's last name.

The next day, everyone was out doing stuff, so I went to the beach with Matthew. I sat by the ocean. Was Ezra dead? Was Ezra alive? Matthew asked me if he could go into the water.

"Yes, but be careful."

Matthew walked slowly off the shallow sand and into the surf. *Holy cow!* I said in my head. *The waves out there are crazy big!* I saw Matthew keep strutting into the sea. He was so far out that the waves were up to his waist. *Oh no*, I thought, *that's gonna knock him down!* There was an enormous wave coming straight for him.

"Matthew!" I yelled. "Come back!" But he didn't hear me. A wave pushed Matthew underwater, and his head fell back. What was I supposed to do? I couldn't swim!

"Security! Security! Help!" I yelled. It was just then that I realized that the clouds above me had turned dark. It started sprinkling. Then showering. Then pouring. Then it stormed. The rain pounded down on me as I stood helplessly, watching Matthew struggle. Yeah, he could swim, but every time he popped up, a wave pushed him back down. Thunder crashed in the sky. Finally, a security guard saw me and rushed over.

"He's stuck," I said.

The guard dove into the water and grabbed Matthew. He swam back up to the surface and let Matthew go.

"Th-thanks." Matthew coughed up seawater.

Chapter 16

CORBIN

I took Matthew inside a local Dairy Queen.

"What are we gonna do here?" he asked.

"Let me call Will," I said. "Then we can go from there." I dialed his number, but he didn't answer. "OK, he didn't answer. Let's just stay here for a minute." I was walking up to get some food when I heard my phone ring. I answered; it was Will.

"Sorry I missed you," he said. "What's up?"

"Matthew might have to see a doctor," I said. "He almost drowned."

"Oh man. Yeah, you probably should."

About an hour later, I was sitting by Matthew's chair when the doctor walked into the room and told us what needed to be done to heal him. Then he left. On a nearby countertop, I noticed a stack of papers with the words "Ezra Woods" at the top.

I wondered what that meant. Was it a hospital bill? That was the most reasonable guess. I continued to read and saw some more interesting things.

Ezra Woods
- Body reaction expected from surge
- Body being held in special test lab 29

I wondered what this meant. They couldn't be holding his body in lab 29 right now. We were in lab 29. Where was he? I stood up to get a better look at the paper. I rested my hand on the countertop, and a cupboard opened.

"Whoa …" Matthew said. "It's a passageway."

I hesitantly crawled through the little opening. Soon the ceiling raised and I could stand. I walked a little farther and I saw him floating in midair. He wore nothing except the gym shorts he had been wearing when he died. I assumed this was how they were performing tests on his body. Lightning streaks floated around him. His head hung back, and his eyes were shut. Tubes ran down from his chest and into a desk. What did it mean? I walked over to the desk. On it was a large glowing blue button and a paper taped to it that said: "Do not press until Septaday 31. Will be revived."

I didn't fully understand what this meant. I carefully removed the paper and then hesitantly pressed down on the button. Blue lightning burst through the tubes and into Ezra's body. He started flinching and sparking all over! After about ten seconds, his body dropped and made a hole in the ground. I walked over and looked down the hole. A huge lightning bolt shot up from his body, out of the hole, through the roof, and into the sky. About fifteen seconds later, the lightning stopped. I looked back down into the hole. Ezra lay there with his eyes open.

"C-Corbin?" he asked weakly.

"Ezra! You're back?"

Ezra closed his eyes and smiled. He was really back.

Part 3

REVIVED

Chapter 17

EZRA

Hey. It was me. Ezra. I was back. Not dead. You know, the more I thought about it, since I was fourteen years old, it was really annoying that I had just died, had my birthday, and came back to life.

As Corbin and I walked down the hallway, we noticed faint screams coming from ahead. We walked on until we were outside the room from which the screams emanated. I slammed open the door. Inside was a kid about my age. He was getting stabbed by an electric staff.

"Hey!" I yelled. "Get off him!" I shot a bolt at the man's head.

"*Ahh*!" The man fell to the ground. Corbin and I quickly untied the kid and helped him out the door.

"What's your name?" I asked.

"Kolby. Kolby Rodgers."

"Why were they doing that?" I asked.

He sighed. "They think I have information, so they just took me off the streets. But I don't know anything."

"Whoa," said Corbin.

After saving this random kid, I felt different. What would he do? More importantly, what could I do to help him? I had no idea who this kid was. I couldn't really do anything, could I? Or could I? Wait …

If I could, I would help him, I concluded. But when? What would I do? Escape the people that were helping me? Was this kid on my side? Against the DM?

Later that same day, we got a call from a Phoenix Protection Center, and they asked if we would come by for an hour or two. Of course, we accepted, but only me, Corbin, Elijah, and Will went. About an hour and a half later, we arrived at a dry, empty stretch of land. Out in the open was a gate. Past the gate was a little house. Not too little but not greatly big. There was also a big yard with tents, cameras, and computers. Six fancy cars were parked in the driveway. They were cars that I knew from Earth. It was weird having cars from Earth in a different universe. I wondered how that was possible.

Two guards stood at the entrance. They let us in without a word.

"Holy cow!" Corbin exclaimed. "Look at those cars!"

We walked into the house and were greeted by a tall man wearing a black fancy tux. We entered a room with a large table.

"Here, sit. Sit down," the man said.

After a few minutes of talking, I got a call on my phone. I hung up without answering.

"Sorry about that," I apologized.

"Uh … what number was that?" Will asked hesitantly.

"*Um* …" I looked at my recent calls. "It's just all zeros."

His face went white, and his eyes widened. "*Um.* Can I see your phone for a sec?"

"Sure." I gave him my phone. I wondered what this was all about. Will left the room. I continued talking to the man.

"Can I see the restroom?" I asked.

"Sure. It's right down the hall."

"Thanks."

As I walked toward it, I saw Will in the hallway, talking on the phone.

"Please can you hold it off?" He begged. He paused. "Please? Come on. I can get the money for you by Doubaday." Another short pause. Then he hung up.

"What's that all about?" I asked.

He spun around. He hadn't known I was there.

"*Um* ... nothing."

"No, Will. Tell me what it is."

He sighed. "I've been living by the government since I was three. You know how in this universe you can see what's going on in other universes? Well, they know how the government has helped me for ten years, and now since I'm here, they're demanding a fee."

That was how they had cars from Earth; they could see us. But this was astonishing news. I told him we'd figure it out, and just before I opened the door to talk to the alien man, the windows around us shattered. I ran out of the building when I saw a weird movement and glass break on one of the cars. I stared at the car and then walked back inside. What was that? Was there something in the car? Why did the window break?

The tall guy in the tux said, "I have gathered you all here to talk about something very important. Ezra, that kid you met, did he seem a little strange?"

I thought for a moment and then replied, "Maybe a little."

He said, "We've known this kid for quite a while now, and we know his purpose. He's with us. He has powers like you. We invited you here to develop a plan to rescue him from the horrible place he's in."

Then I realized that there was something familiar about that kid. I had seen him when we first arrived in this universe!

Chapter 18

EZRA

My mind froze. I couldn't take this much stress and pressure. It was overwhelming.

"Now, Kolby, the kid you met, is friends with kids named Simon Smith, Logan Lee, Gabe Diamond, Kyler Mount, Zachary, and Jase Tip. These are the last known humans in this world. They have been here for five months. We don't have any idea how they got here," the man explained.

I thought and thought about it. How could this have happened?

A few hours after the meeting, we returned to the house. I saw Kolby and some other kids standing by my other friends.

"This is my cousin, Simon," Kolby said. "And this is Kyler, Logan, Gabe, Zach, and Jase. As humans here, we all have powers too." He pointed to them as he talked.

"Nice to meet you," I said. "Welcome to the clan."

Chapter 19

ezra

The Powered Humans—A Phoenix Resource

- Ezra Woods
- Corbin Kennly
- Will Tale
- Elijah Hart
- Madison Holt
- Abigail Kennly
- Brinx Right
- Simon Smith
- Logan Lee
- Gabe Diamond
- Kyler Lade
- Zachary Ites
- Jase Ites

- Bryce Woods
- Matthew Woods

The Phoenix Force

- Julian Phoenix
- Colvin Phoenix

I knew there were a lot of powered kids, yet I never realized just how many. Yes, I knew all of them, but I completely forgot how many people there were. Wow. Fifty-two. How had I never realized this? Then I woke from the dream.

OK. Only seventeen. *Phew.* Will told me how I had fallen asleep. Apparently since I had risen, I lost energy very quickly. This was going to be permanent. Clearly dying and rising again was going to ruin the rest of my life. Crud.

Why exactly was the paper sitting there? I told everyone that I questioned why the paper was there. We all brainstormed a reason. There was no possible answer.

The next day, there was a knock on the door. I opened it up and saw an alien man that looked like he was in his twenties. He had slicked-back green hair and wore a dress shirt. It was the guy from the Phoenix Protection Center.

"We would like to show you some of the production we have been working on."

"Totally," I replied.

As we arrived at the Phoenix Protection Center, we were stunned by a huge castle wall. The navy blue wall stretched for what looked like seven hundred feet. On top of the wall was a walkway with glowing orange railings. In the middle was a glowing blue streak of light down the center of the wall. Behind the rails was a door. The door led into a navy-and-orange castle. The castle had many cannons and looked like a place prepared to battle.

"The Phoenix Force is coming," the man said, "and we're using this tower to prepare. Would you like to help us?"

"Of course!" I said. This could be the chance I needed.

We had begun a tour of the castle when suddenly the sky turned purple and the clouds turned red. We heard the sound of marching feet approaching. Planes roaring through the sky in the distance. It was the Phoenix Force.

Chapter 20

EZRA

Our army was short, with barely over two thousand people. The Phoenix army topped four thousand.

I went into a private room with my friends.

"OK, guys. This is it. This is what it all comes down to. Corbin and Kyler, I want you inside the rocker robot. Brinx, I want you to fight from here. If I didn't say your name, you're on the battlefield with me unless told otherwise. Got it?"

"Yes," everyone said in unison.

The Phoenix army marched on. But after long, they came to a stop in front of the building. Not one word. Everything was quiet.

"Now," Dr. Phoenix said in a loud voice. His words echoed throughout the land. "Let's fight."

The DM army ran toward the wall. Our army ran at the DM, prepared for battle. A chorus of screams sounded. My friends and I were in the middle of the battlefield. The rocker robot looked like a spider in the form of a machine. Corbin picked up a guy from the rocker and threw him. Just then a spear flew toward my head. I ducked just in time. I threw a lightning ball at one of the aliens.

"Ezra!" Gabe yelled. "Look!" He pointed at the sky.

A plane carrying a bomb was approaching. But I wouldn't worry about that. Out of the corner of my eye, I saw Kolby get pinned to the ground. I shocked him with a bolt of lightning. There was so much chaos. Then I saw Corbin save Madi from an alien. One of these times, it was not going to go our way.

I gathered my friends and went to a safe spot where nobody could see us.

"We need a new plan," Jase said.

"This is not how I imagined it," Elijah said.

"Why don't we just go to the base and shoot cannons and stuff from there?" Logan suggested.

"I think we have to do that," I said.

We entered the castle. We ran to the railings and used our abilities to fight from there.

"Me and Brinx are gonna go down a story and gather some weapons," said Zach.

"OK," I said. "Be careful."

"Do you know where the weapons even are?" Zach asked.

"No idea. Maybe we can ask someone."

"Excuse me," Brinx said. "Can you point us toward the weapons rack?"

"Sure," said a green-faced alien.

Just then a loud explosion burst into the sky and castle.

"Look out!" Zach screamed.

Crumbled rocks flew down toward the ground.

"Run!"

Everyone scattered.

All of a sudden, Phoenix's men came out of nowhere. They invaded the castle fully armed. Meanwhile, Zach and Brinx ran back to the barriers at the edge of the castle.

"Ezra!" Brinx yelled. "Come quick! We are being overtaken!"

"What?" I said.

"How is that possible?" Corbin said.

"Hurry up! Let's go!"

We all followed Brinx and Zach down the stairs. There must have been a dozen Phoenix men waiting for us. We tried to go back, but we were cornered.

Will said, "I can take them on."

All of a sudden, he shot a big beam of light. It almost knocked all of them out.

"Go on!" said Will. He cleared the bottom half of the men. We ran down the stairs as fast as we could. Will stayed at the top.

"Will!" I screamed. "Come on!"

From the corner of my eye, I saw Will get hit in the head with a blue laser. I was infuriated with them, but I couldn't go back because there were too many men. I would never forget this day. The day that the Phoenix Force took my friend.

Chapter 21

EZRA

I turned toward the top of the stairs, but Madison and Elijah tugged on the back of my shirt. It was no use. I saw Will's body fall. Half of me wanted to cry; the other half wanted to kill Dr.

We looked for an exit, but it was no use. All the exits were blocked with debris from the bomb. Just when we thought it couldn't get any worse, we heard a whooshing sound and hundreds of grenades dropped onto the castle. Smoke and fire surrounded us while rocks fell. Flames tore down the castle until there was nothing left. As the castle walls fell, the fire and smoke died down. Madi had generated a force field and covered us just in time. As we walked away from the destroyed castle, we looked at the battlefield. What was before us was madness. But we were here. Better than ever.

I ran into battle. There was fighting at every angle. Portals to different universes opened everywhere. I saw Bryce fighting a monster. But then I saw something really ... weird. A four-armed monster approached us. He had to be at least twelve feet tall. Simon and his friends just stared at him with dirty looks on their faces. Did they know him?

Simon threw green lightning at the monster. Logan picked him up and threw him down to the ground. The monster stood up and grabbed Zach by the neck. He threw him, but Madi saved him from a hard landing with a force field. The war shifted over, so we were now just in a flat landed plain. The war was just about fifty feet away from us now. I saw a plane soar above us and land only about a hundred feet away. Three people hopped out and approached us. As they got closer, I suddenly realized who they were. The Phoenix Force were coming.

Chapter 22

EZRA

Soon enough, I could see every Phoenix Force member. Virgil, Colvin, and Julian Phoenix.

"How is Phoenix on a plane? I thought he was fighting," I said.

"I saw the plane pick him up," Corbin responded.

When they were close enough to us, Dr. Phoenix tied all of us to the ground with lightning.

"This is it," he said. "We've finally caught you. You shouldn't have known about the multiverse. It's too big for all of you to handle. And now it's time to go away."

"------Xahsgwhdvb. __He---lllo-. ... Par__=//`Don-", ThE-- INTER__U=PTION Ca---ll__ ME_-_+=-+-__+_(_)Th==_E VO---IC_E. ____-=--__-.""

Dr. Phoenix was squeezing us down to the ground so hard that I antigenerated with my friends. I didn't care where we went; we just needed to get away. We antigenerated to the top of a bridge with a blackened substance under it. I looked to the side. The Phoenix Force had antigenerated with us.

"Get all the Woods first," Dr. Phoenix, pointing his finger at us. About half a dozen of his troopers stood behind him.

"No!" Elijah screamed. Matthew, Bryce, and I shielded ourselves. "Take me first."

"Hey," said a voice behind Dr. Phoenix. the doctor turned around.

I couldn't believe who it was: Will Tale. But he wasn't in human form. It was more ghostly.

Dang, we were glad to see him.

He shot a light beam right at Dr. Phoenix's face. The doctor screamed as he hit the ground. Will took the troopers out with a force field. Just then, Dr. Phoenix woke up, knocked me down, pointed his finger straight at Madi, and shot lightning from it. Madison deflected with a force field that shot back at my face.

"Ezra! Are you OK?" she asked.

"I'm good," I muttered back. I turned my hand into pure lightning and smacked Dr. Phoenix on the head. It left a nasty bruise on his forehead. I swung at him again, but he dodged it. Then I punched him, this time in the lip. He fell to the ground.

I looked at my friends, and they all looked at me. It was one of the greatest things I'd ever seen. Bryce and Matthew ran up and hugged me. Everyone started cheering and high-fiving.

Just then, Dr. Phoenix's flowing purple electricity divided us by about six to seven feet. This guy never went away.

"I need the girl. I need the little ones. And … I need the Woods." He used his force to pull Madi, Bryce, and Matthew toward him, but I didn't dare budge. It was I felt as if I were paralyzed

"Fine," Dr. Phoenix said. "You don't have to come. Because you won't live to come." He blasted me with a purple fire beam as hot as 2,600–3,000 degrees Fahrenheit. The only way I could survive was to surge so the lightning would throw off the fire.

"*Ahh!*" I screamed.

"I won't stop until you come to me," he scolded.

I screamed and screamed again.

"Stop it! You're killing him!" Madi yelled.

"Stop it!" Bryce screamed.

"He's gonna die … again!" Matthew exclaimed.

"What are you doing?" I yelled.

"What I need to do."

At that moment, I knew I looked as if he was going to explode me. And Dr. Phoenix was still tugging on me over and over to come with him.

"Watch out," I said weakly to Madi and my friends. "Watch out."

A brilliant idea suddenly popped into my mind. And just in the nick of time! It was as if were play tug-of-war and I let go of the rope or the other person or team tell. If I let Dr. Phoenix take me, his pulling pressure would knock him down!

As I let go, I slammed right into Bryce, but Dr. Phoenix fell back. As he got back up, he shot a bolt at my head. I fell back. I was super dizzy, and Dr. Phoenix antigenerated away with Elijah, Madi, and Brinx. As I looked back to my friends, I noticed Bryce was getting attacked by a trooper. Bryce wasn't conscious! His head drooped off the side of the bridge.

"Nooo!" I screamed.

"Say goodbye," the trooper said as he pushed Bryce off the bridge.

I didn't have any reaction time. I jumped off the bridge while knocking the trooper back into the substance too. I reached out my hand. Then I saw a bolt of lightning come down to us. I grabbed and threw more down to Bryce. He grabbed onto it too. We were desperately hanging for our lives. The lightning rope reeled us back up. We were safe.

I turned around toward the rest of my friends.

"We have to go find them."

I was sitting at Vadg's long table, thinking of a plan to rescue my friends, when my phone rang. I checked it. It was the government. They were calling for Will. I answered.

"Where is Will Tale?"

"He died during the war."

"Yeah right. We need the money. Now who will pay for it?"

Just then there was a knock on the door and a bright light flashed outside.

"Hold on one sec," I said into the phone. I opened the door. On the porch was Will and he held a package in his hand. I blinked and he was gone, but the package wasn't. I picked up the package and read its label:

> To: Ezra Woods
> From: Will Tale

Is Will still alive? I wondered. I read on:

> Inside here is something you might need. You know the elementals, time, space, atmosphere, galaxy, and soul? Well, inside this package is the time element, though it will need to be powered. Use this and don't let anyone get it. Also, there are some semielements in there too. There is lightning for you and light to remember me by. There is also money for the government.
>
> Thank you for being my friend, forever and always, dead or alive.
>
> —Will Tale

I looked straight ahead. When had he made this? There were so many questions in my head that needed answers. *When did he make this?* I repeated to myself. I had the craziest feelings I'd ever felt. I went into the backyard and started to play basketball. Will was one of the only people who would actually play basketball with me. I took a three-pointer from the spot from which Will would always shoot. *Swish. For Will*, I said in my head. *For Will.*

Chapter 23

EZRA

Time passed after the war and Will's death. I had been studying ways to find my friends. One of them was by using antigenerate. But I had no idea where the DM was holding them or how to get past the antigenerate barrier. Another way was to use the time machine, but it would take a while to make a new one. A third method was the time element. Will said it needed to be fully powered though.

I looked at the time elemental amulet in my hand. I was thinking of ways to charge it. I stared at the amulet intensely, and it took on a greenish glow. I closed my eyes. How would I ever power it? I walked outside and looked far out onto the horizon

"___--+==It---I__s The__-/.Voi*5-ce I /?' Know--- Wha-t You@4gh=Are/// Suff/{[}'_ering. @#!37_B!@#e<,,Rea---_\dy;; For||@ War_____--_--_-@@#!bellum

_ peace"

I remember that *bellum* means war. Just then, I heard Bryce call me.

"What is it?" I yelled.

"Something's happening!"

I ran over to Bryce. I looked in my hand. The time amulet was glowing as if it was activated. Everything in the room was lifting into the air, seemingly magically.

"What's going on?" he asked.

"I don't know," I said back. "I think it's powering up."

A giant green explosion suddenly knocked me to the floor. I regained consciousness almost immediately. It was like everything was back to normal. We were back on Earth, but it didn't feel right; it felt like we were in a paradox. A paradox on the multiverse.

Chapter 24

EZRa

Two and a Half Months Later

Hey, my name was Ezra Woods. If you hadn't heard of me, here are a few things about me to get you started:

- I possess elemental superpowers.
- I live with my friends in a different universe.
- I fought a one-on-one battle with evil billionaire Dr. Virgil Phoenix.
- My best friend, Will, sacrificed himself so we could live.
- I fought in a world-against-world war.

All my friends had powers too, along with my two seven-year-old brothers, Bryce and Matthew Woods. Bryce has a connection through eternity. He is basically the most powerful being the multiverse will ever have. Matthew has a smooth and flowing lightning-fire tube. He also has a Spidermanlike lightning tube.

Everyone's powers were as follows.

- Me—lightning
- Corbin—fire
- Elijah—water and weather
- Madi—force field
- Abi—mind control
- Brinx—thermal energy
- Simon—super speed
- Logan—lightning and force
- Gabe—ice
- Kyler—elastic
- Zach—
- Jase—flight
- Bryce—eternity and portal
- Matthew—lightning tubes

"We're in some sort of paradox," I said. There weren't many houses, but there were a lot of Phoenix Force flags.

"I think Phoenix has taken over," said Bryce.

"Yeah, no kidding," said Matthew.

My first thought was to get to my house. I wondered if it had been destroyed. By the way it looked, many houses had been destroyed. We soon started to think about all the other elements Will had talked about.

"Let me check my watch to see where we are." I turned on my watch and assessed the location app. "We are near my house; we just need to take a left."

We ran down the street to find four Phoenix men patrolling the street. One of them spotted us.

"Hey!" they shouted.

We ran back the other way. Soon, we hit a dead end. We were

ready to fight. One of them shot a bullet at me, and I barely dodged it. I shot a lightning bolt at them, and it hit. It caused some sort of chain reaction and shocked all four of the men.

We successfully got past them, ran straight to my house, and finally settled down.

Chapter 25

EZRa

The next day, I told everyone about the elemental amulets.

"That's awesome," said Bryce.

"How many did you say there was, Ezra?" Corbin asked.

"There are five multiverse elements in total," I said. "Right now, I only have one, but we have two of the semielements, light and lightning."

I thought for a moment. "We need to find the rest of them. We need to split into groups. Corbin, Abi, Bryce, and Matthew, come exploring with me. Simon, Logan, Gabe, Zach, Jase, and Kyler, you guys, fortify the base," I announced.

Suddenly, there was a knock on the door. I peeked out the window and saw Phoenix men outside. Usually I wouldn't be nervous, but this time was different. The men looked loaded. They wore masks and protection gear as if they were ready for battle. They had gray laser shooters with barrels that glowed red and white. It looked like a laser-energy mix. They didn't look like they were here to play.

They banged more loudly on the door.

"Quick, hide," I whispered to the others.

I opened the door and saw five Phoenix men towering over me. I said in a British accent, "Hello. Welcome to my house. Is there anything you need?" I really tried not to act suspicious.

"We are here to inspect your house. We have orders, sir," one of the men replied.

They just started marching inside the house without any regard. They checked the bathroom, cabinets, and bedrooms. "Clear," one of them said.

"See, sir. There is nothing to see here," I said happily.

Just then, a loud vibrating bang came from up the stairs. The guards exchanged suspicious looks. At the exact moment, they all rushed upstairs. I followed quickly behind them. One of the men was looking under the bed when a tube of yellowish orange lightning shot at his face. Matthew crawled out from under the bed and stood up. Soon all of us started to dart outside.

As we ran out of the house, I looked to my side and asked Matthew, "What was that for?"

"It's just a reflex," he said as he gasped for air. "I can't help it."

Soon we were all in the backyard, ready to fight.

Chapter 26

EZRA

I was the first to shoot. I missed him, but he also missed me. I turned around to see the fence burning.

"Whoa!" said Bryce.

"The lasers just catch anything they hit on fire," said Corbin.

Bam! All of a sudden, I saw a fire laser shoot at Corbin. It shot straight through him! He didn't even flinch. His body started to glow.

"Corbin, somethings happening!" I shouted.

Boom! An explosion knocked all of us back. The Phoenix men were knocked unconscious. Corbin was somehow OK! He wasn't burned or bruised! We all got back up and went back inside. We started to hear static. It was a radio transmitter from one of the Phoenix men. It was Dr. Phoenix. We listened in closely.

****Guard*s**repo-rt for**duty**the**second********
amulet**is**on**the**coast****of*Puerto Rico******in*a*
rainforest**in a temple.*****It**is*the**atmosphere**amulet***

I stood there, stunned. Soon after, I called to my friends, "Pack your bags! We're going to Puerto Rico!"

"What?" Ezra asked. "Puerto Rico?"

"You're starting to get a little crazy," Zach said.

"Yeah, Ezra. That's impossible."

"Guys," I said. "It's where the atmosphere amulet is!"

"How are we even going to get there?" Logan asked.

I looked at Phoenix's empty mansion. When the time amulet exploded, had Phoenix come back to Earth with us?

"There can't be anyone in Phoenix's house," I said. "But there has to be money. Maybe we can buy plane tickets with Phoenix's money."

Everyone looked at each other.

"Well?" I said.

"We're in," Corbin replied.

Phoenix's house was insanely big. I busted open the doors. Steel plates covered the floor. We searched everywhere for a trace of money. No luck. I saw Corbin's jaw drop.

"What?" I said.

"You'll never believe this," he replied.

I looked onto the counter. Eight plane tickets to Puerto Rico were sitting there.

"No way," I said in astonishment. "I bet Phoenix was planning to go to Puerto Rico to get the amulet before he time traveled. He probably had five extra for guards."

"Which eight of us are going?" Corbin asked me.

"It depends which superpowers would be more useful," I replied. "I need everyone over here!" I called out.

"We have eight tickets," I said to my friends. "So only eight people can go. Now who's it going to be?"

"To start, I think Ezra should go. Along with Simon, Corbin, Matthew, Bryce, and Zach." said Abigail.

Everyone agreed.

"Then probably … Logan and Kyler," Gabe said.

Everyone agreed again.

"OK," I said. "Let's get moving."

Chapter 27

ezra

Five days later …

"Are we there yet?" asked Matthew, waking up.

"Yes, we are," I proudly announced. I looked out the plane window. The sun was setting, and its bright light shined for miles. It was a beautiful sight among the forest of trees.

"I booked us a large house with Vadg's AIPM card that he gave us," I said to my friends. AIPM stood for Advanced Instant PayMent.

"Bro, that's insane," Mathew said. "I wish I had one of my own. I could be a billionaire! But … not … well … yeah, not Phoenix."

We all frowned. "Heartbreak Hotel" started playing on the radio. I felt tears fall. Oh no. Hopefully nobody aboard the plane got the wrong idea, because I was the only one crying.

Yes, I missed Will, but I was a man now. And I had to lead my team to what was best for us and what was best for the rest of the world.

The plane landed with all large *whoosh*. As we deplaned, and I thought I saw something. A man driving a 1997 Honda Civic. The car was not well taken care of, as evidenced by the dents in its doors. The man's face was bandaged as if he had been in a serious accident. His face looked though he was hiding something. Suddenly, the plane burst into flames just as I was about to hop out.

"Bryce!" I yelled. "Jump out!"

Bryce jumped out of the plane just in the nick of time. We looked back as it exploded because the flames had reached a fuel tank. I saw a black substance that looked like oil pouring out of the plane. If that was what it was, we were in for a ride. The goo was slick and moist, and it seemed be creeping toward us. Then the goo made a ... scream? A split second later, everything went black. I tried to open my eyes but couldn't. An image popped into my head. Me and my friends were outside, all having fun. It seemed like we were getting along better than we did now. One weird thing was that Will was still alive. We were all playing soccer outside, and I just felt joy. It felt like a fantasy but a reality at the same time. The thought swirled in my mind. What if he was still alive?

There was something different about all my friends. I couldn't tell what it was, though. It was just a feeling. Suddenly, the sky went dark, and it looked like a thunderstorm was approaching. Everyone looked at me. It started to rain lightly. Will reached out his hand toward me, but then he just dissolved into ash. One by one, the same thing happened to the rest of my friends until I was the only one left, standing in the pouring rain, all alone.

A few seconds later, I heard screaming and a ringing in my ear. Then I woke up. The goo was clinging to Bryce's arm. It kept on screaming. I wanted to try something, so with all my might, I shot lightning out of my hand right at the goo. It froze for a second.

In shock, we ran over to Bryce. His arm was bleeding. Then we saw little shards. Could it be the amulet, or was it maybe just glass? Then the shards started to glow. My friends and I studied his arm. Soon, his whole arm was glowing! Then his arm and the goo disintegrated into ash. It wasn't fast; it was slow like when I would get a snack from the store. By the time the goo was gone, Bryce was still there, just not all of him.

"We need to get him to a hospital or a lab now," said a voice coming from the plane.

This had happened before with a voice always talking in the background. I didn't think this could be anyone else except the … Voice.

Chapter 28

EZRA

"8h$eIIo 9i@s my signal getting clear. Hello, I haven't had a formal introduction, my name is Voice>@>. I sometimes interact with Ezra and his friends or maybe not. I may be a mysterious ch)racter or not you will never know, By the way (r&*Br#y$c#r%i&!@'may not make it hah^4h*&*ha^$a^&*h hahaha-#&ha5trfHAHAHA)*&+$&/',. *Signal could not be reached*"

So now we had this information about the Voice. But was it on our side or not?

Who would we tell about this possibly mysterious character? That's what it said. Right? Did anyone else have more information? What would we do with the information it gave us?

Two hours passed. So far we had made it to a lab, and they thought Bryce's arm was dissolving because of the shards. The one thing that was strange was that if the time amulet had indeed activated, I would have shards in my arm too because I was near him when it happened. The doctor said I was right. Next, we needed to remove the shards out of his arm. There was only one problem: They couldn't remove all the shards. They could only remove three, which would leave one. So far I had been waiting in the waiting room, but then, out of nowhere, Corbin came running out the door to Bryce's room and said, "Bryce is OK! He's now stable."

"What about the last shard?" I asked. "Did they get it out?"

"No, because if they take it out, he could die."

"What will the shard do to his body?"

"The doc said he may have the power of time but that when he uses his power, he slowly dies, so he must not use his power unless we need it."

Chapter 29

EZRA

I walked into Bryce's room. He did not look good.

"And you said he'll be fine?" I asked the doctor.

"Yes," the doctor replied. "Unless you take the last shard out. The last shard is the most powerful because it's the biggest. It's the only thing keeping him alive."

This was all happening so fast. I didn't know what to do. Go after Phoenix or wait for Bryce. I discussed what I could do with my friends, and they said to wait for Bryce. I walked back into Bryce's room. The main doctor and another doctor sat at a desk. The second doctor stared at me secretly from behind his computer.

"How long is this supposed to take?" I asked the main doctor.

"A few days. Maybe more if he has any reactions," he replied.

"What are the reactions?" I questioned.

Almost immediately, the other doctor at the desk spoke up: "Low or high heart rate, headaches, arm pain, tiredness, and if it gets really bad, he could have temporary faints."

Everyone in the room looked at the doctor at the desk.

"Get back to work," the main doctor said in a stern but questionable voice. I looked at Bryce, and he looked pretty worried. Just then, I heard a sound coming from the sky. I looked out the window and saw an orange-and-purple helicopter with the letters PF on it. Oh no. I looked back to the room.

"What's wrong?" the doctor said, worried.

I wasn't focused on his question. I was focused on the man at the desk. He was still staring at me but now with an evil grin stretching across his face. He was an undercover Phoenix man. He had led the Phoenix Force right to us.

"Go!" I yelled. Just then, the roof caved in. The floor cracked under my feet, and I slid through. Within seconds, the building was covered in flames. Firefighters rushed to the building. I barely got out with my life.

"Where's Bryce?" Corbin yelled.

"I don't know! The floor caved in, and I couldn't find him! I'm hoping a firefighter will find him," I replied.

After five minutes, my brother was nowhere to be seen.

"That's it!" I yelled. "I'm going in!"

"Ezra! No!" Corbin screamed.

I ran into the flames. Wood and pieces of concrete lay on the ground. I looked up to the floor Bryce was on. It was barely standing. I climbed and jumped up onto bars and anything I could hold onto to get up. I was almost to Bryce's floor when I realized a problem. There was a bar hanging from his window. I was about sixty feet up in the air. I could jump to the bar or plummet to the ground. It was the only way to get to Bryce.

I looked through Bryce's window and saw him struggling to get his arm out of the holder. I had to save him. With all the strength in my legs, I jumped. My fingers touched the metal bar. I tried to hang on for my life, but my fingers slipped and I fell deep into the fire. A split-second later, Bryce's arm started to glow with the power of time activated, and my friends and I went back five minutes in time.

Chapter 30

BRYCE

"Ezra! Where are you?" I screamed.

Hold on. First I wanted to get this clear: this was my way of the story. My name was Bryce Woods, and I had just seen my brother jump up to my burning hospital window and fall sixty feet down into fire. I had no idea what to do. If you're wondering why this happened, I wouldn't blame you.

A helicopter had dropped a bomb on the hospital we were in. Everyone scattered and left me helpless. My hand was being held up in a cast sort of thing that was connected to the ceiling. When everyone fled, I was left with my arm stuck. I couldn't get it out no matter how hard I tried. My brother, Ezra, had gotten tired of waiting and came to rescue me. He climbed to the top of the burning building and tried to jump to my window. He slipped and fell into the fire. I was doomed.

What could I do? Well, if Ezra could make a chain reaction

with the fire and his lightning, we might be able to escape safely, I pondered.

That was when I noticed something. The Honda Civic from the airport was sitting there, all dented and banged up. The glass had been shattered from the bomb. But then I noticed something else. The man's clothes were torn and burned all over, and there was goo in the car.

All of the sudden, I reversed time with my arm, and we were zooming back to before the bomb was dropped. All the cars were fine, and there was no fire. I decided we would prevent the bomb from dropping onto the hospital this time. *This could be hard*, I thought. It seemed impossible to convince everyone to leave. They'd pay with their lives, right? If they didn't believe me, they would end up dying.

After I got a couple people to leave the hospital by bribing them, the Honda Civic pulled up, but the glass was already shattered. I could also clearly see goo all over the car. I knew an alien had attacked the car. Then I noticed the man who was driving the car was bleeding out yellow blood. I could tell that he was not human or even the typical alien.

He parked the car and sat down on the hood. Just then, the back of his shirt ripped, and a huge horn came out. He was an alien. The car's hood got crushed and was never to be seen again, or so I thought. It then crushed the car sitting a few stories below me. Each part of the car kept exploding and flying in every direction, hitting other cars and destroying them. One went through a window in the building and crashed into an empty hospital gurney. The man got off the car, which was now just a chassis, and got onto another car, shattering the glass under his weight. He kept jumping from one car to the next, shattering the glass every time. He was almost as destructive as the bomb.

Right after the last car had been destroyed, I heard a *whoosh*. I looked up and saw the helicopter hovering. It was coming for us.

"Hey, Ezra ..." I said. "See that helicopter there? Well, we might want to get away from it."

"What?" he said, confused. He looked at the helicopter.

"A bomb is going to drop in a couple of seconds!" I yelled at the top of my lungs. "Ezra! Do something!"

There was no way Ezra would listen to me. He never listened to me back home. I needed proof that the bomb was going to drop and that the helicopter was Phoenix Force. I looked at the helicopter. Every Phoenix Force helicopter came standard with multiple sets of landing gear.

"Hey, Ezra. Do you see the six holes that the wheels come out of?"

"Yes, why?"

"Most helicopters only have three holes, while the Phoenix Force's have six. This could be a huge problem, depending on how they use them. Ezra, you know what we have to do?"

"I need more proof than that," he said.

"Ezra, try shooting lightning at it!"

"I can't. What if it's not the Phoenix Force? What if they're innocent?"

"We have to take a chance. If you won't do it, I will. I get that you're my big brother and the leader, but if these people are actually on his side, hundreds could die."

"Fine. If you want to do it, do it, but I am not responsible for your mistakes." He got my arm out of the sling, and we all ran outside.

"OK, let's do this," I say. "First I will freeze the helicopter in air and then you will take them down."

"All right, but if it isn't the Phoenix Force, you're in a lot of trouble, Bryce."

"Dude, do you really think I would put innocent people in danger?"

"That's true, but you are my little brother and if something bad were to happen, this could go terribly wrong. And you would harm innocents in an accident. How am I supposed to know that you can do this?" Ezra said.

"You have to trust me, Ezra. This is important. You are always the leader. Let me take this role just this time," I pleaded.

He thought about it and said, "OK, little bro. Let's do this!"

I looked at Ezra, Corbin, Simon, and everyone else. Then I looked at the helicopter. This was a big risk.

"We could send someone up there?" I suggested.

"That's true," Abi said. "We could blast someone up there."

"I can go if you want," Simon said.

"OK, we're going to have to shock you," Ezra replied.

"I can take that," Simon said confidently.

"OK. On the count of three. One, two, three!" Ezra shot a bolt of lightning at Simon's feet, and Simon flew into the sky and landed on the side of the helicopter.

"Oh shoot!" Simon said to himself. "This is not good."

He hung off the side of a helicopter and slowly shifted toward the front. He planned to blast open the windshield. As he was climbing, his hand started to sweat.

"Not good," he muttered. When he neared the front of the helicopter, he punched his lightning fist into the window. The glass shattered and fell toward the ground.

"Ah!" the pilot screamed. "Attacker!"

"He's after the bomb!" one of them said.

"Well, do something!" another said.

"What's going on?" I heard yet another voice. A man walked in from the back. He wore a mask and a protection suit.

"Mr. Wayne! Sir, we have an attacker!"

"Set it on self-destruct mode and jump out!" the man ordered.

Soon, they all jumped out one by one. Simon looked at the bomb and saw a horrible sight. A bright red countdown started for three minutes. The bomb was about two feet wide and two feet tall.

He called Ezra.

"Hello?" Ezra said. "What happened?"

"Houston, we have a problem.

"What! What happened? And why did I see the people on the plane jump out?" Ezra yelled worriedly.

"When I got inside the helicopter, the pilot set the bomb on self-destruct mode and jumped out!"

"*Um* ... can you try to steer the helicopter away from the city and the hospital? Let it explode in a field or something?"

"I can try," Simon said. He hopped into the pilot seat. "I don't know any of these buttons!" he exclaimed.

"Is there any lever or something that could steer it?"

"*Um* ... yeah, there is."

"OK, just try to maneuver it through things and go to an open space."

"Got it!" Simon put his hand on the lever and started to push forward. Just then, the helicopter started going up and down. "It's getting pretty bumpy," he said uneasily.

"Just keep going. You're doing good!" Ezra said through the phone.

"OK, I got this." Simon said to himself. He smoothly pushed his hand forward and the helicopter straightened out and rode more smoothly.

"OK, there's grassy land coming up. Just keep going forward!"

"Do you know how big the bomb will explode?" Simon asked.

"Corbin, can you run the numbers?" Ezra asked.

"Already done," Corbin said. "Three-quarters of a mile."

The clock hit one minute.

"Only one minute left!" Simon said. "I'm not going to make it!"

"Get a parachute ready! Jump out with around ten seconds left," Ezra brainstormed.

Forty-five seconds. Just then, a beam of red light shot through the helicopter.

"Ezra, what was that?" Simon asked.

"It's Phoenix. They're after us. They're after you."

Another red beam shot through the helicopter's propellers. Twenty seconds left.

"Jump out!" Ezra yelled.

"Oh gosh," Simon said to himself as he looked outside. "This is it."

As the bomb hit ten seconds, Simon jumped. He pulled his parachute rope, and the parachute flew out. He looked back up to the helicopter. It was going to blow any second now. Three, two, one, *boom*. The helicopter exploded with an ear-piercing blow.

"Simon!" Ezra yelled through the phone. "Are you OK?"

We waited a few seconds and then heard, "Yeah, I'm good."

Chapter 31

EZRA

It was Ezra again. Bryce had his turn, but it was mine again.

A few hours after the helicopter thing, my friends and I gathered some money and got two hotel rooms. I really just wanted to be alone. Luckily, I found the best way to do it.

"I'm going to the roof," I said to my friends.

They didn't question why, which was pretty odd. I found the roof access stairs and climbed them. I brought my phone and AirPods with me. I sat down at the edge and watched the busy street below. I connected my AirPods to my phone. "Tell Me Why" started playing.

It reminded me of Will again.

I didn't really think it was a coincidence that this one song started playing right at this exact time. I looked out into space. Then I looked up. The stars shined down brightly on me. The planets and stars were watching me.

I sighed. This song was so good and really had a touching but sad feeling to it.

I wondered if there was someone else out there, listening to this song and thinking about someone they lost.

It made me realize something I'd never thought of before. Maybe Will wanted to die. Maybe he had a smile on his face when he sacrificed himself. Maybe he was happy because he knew, in the long run, that what he did mattered. Only a true friend could do that.

My eyes teared up again. I sprawled out and looked up to the stars again. He was up there, but at the same time he was right beside me. I could feel his presence. He was with me. I never realized what big part of my life he was. He was just a completely innocent kid who saved the life of his friends at the cost of his own. I felt a tear run down my cheek. Then another and another. Would I ever see him again? It didn't seem like it, but I hoped so. I had the rest of my friends, but then why did I feel so alone? Will's death had taken a big piece of me. I was a completely different person without him.

Suddenly, an idea popped into my mind. The time amulet. All I needed was Bryce. If we could figure out a way to go back in time and save Will without getting hurt, we could have him back! And we could finally get a chance to save Madi and Elijah. I ran downstairs and into the hotel room.

"Guys! Guys!" I yelled. Everyone looked at me like something was wrong. "I know how I can save Will! I'm going to see Will again!"

After explaining everything to my friends, I realized something. My little seven-year-old brother could completely change the world. I could save my parents with him. I could save people from dying. He could save people from dying.

"So we're going back in time to save Will?" Kyler asked.

"Yes, and I need your help."

"You need me, don't you?" Bryce said.

"Yeah, I do."

"Do you maybe wanna go back in time and save him right now?" Bryce asked.

"Yeah, let's do this. But, *um* ... how?"

"Trust me. I got this. You want me to send you to the past?"

"Yes. Just do it," I said.

"OK. One rule: you cannot interact with anyone. It will mess up the space time continuum as we know it."

"OK. Let's do it."

Bryce opened a portal to the top of the stairs where Will died. I jumped through the portal and out the other side. The men were lined up, so I snuck behind them without anyone seeing me. I blasted the men with lightning bolts, and they fell forward, down the stairs and onto my friends. With all the chaos, I blasted the men at the bottom too. Will and my friends were safe. I jumped back into the portal. Right then, a shock went through the room. I lay on the ground and so did everyone else. The shock was so powerful, lightning sparked throughout the room and tiny fires started. I heard Bryce groaning on the other side of the room.

"Bryce!" I yelled. I ran toward him. "Bryce, stay with me. Come on. We have to go." I waited a second and said again, "Bryce, come on. Are you good?"

"Can't," I heard him squeak out.

"Come on." I picked him up and put his arm around my shoulder. "You can do this. Come on."

"OK, let's go." He started walking slowly.

It was dark in the room, but the scattered fires lit it up. After about five steps, Bryce fell.

"Bryce, are you OK?" I asked.

He didn't answer.

"Oh shoot," I said to myself. "Come on, Bryce."

"Ezra, it's fine," he said weakly. "Ezra, you have a big chance here. The best way to tell the future is to create it. You have that opportunity. You either make the day or the day makes you."

"No no no. You can't do this. Please don't. Please," I begged.

No response.

"Please, Bryce. This can't be the end."

He closed his eyes. Bryce was gone.

First I lost my best friend and now my brother. I was done. I looked and saw the outline of my friends staring through the fire. It wasn't safe for them to keep fighting. I looked at them. Their faces showed sympathy.

I walked up to Will and said, "Welcome back. We missed you." Then I looked toward the rest of my friends. "Goodbye. Thanks for being my friends."

Matthew looked shocked and scared. Then he started to cry as I walked away.

Chapter 32

EZRA

I ditched my friends. I wish I hadn't. I realize it was likely pretty hard for Will and Matthew. Will probably didn't know what was going on. But Matthew ... well, Matthew had just lost both his brothers in three minutes. I couldn't tell what the heck my friends were thinking. They were going to think I was a chicken for leaving them. Maybe they would try to follow me. I couldn't let them put themselves in danger. Right? I questioned myself, having second thoughts. What would my friends think about me ditching them? If I saw them again, would they forgive me?

No, I ditched them, so ...

I walked away and kept on walking and walking and walking until eventually I reached civilization somewhere.

Their ways of life were different from the other aliens that we—well, I—were with earlier, before I got here.

I stayed in this new city called Indimpoe for quite a while, thinking of all my friends, without me, where I left them, deserted, alone.

But they still had each other. It was not like they completely relied on me. Or had they all looked up to me? What if they had? What would they do without me? Would they join the DM? No. They wouldn't do that! Right?

I was practically dead on the inside, but I hid it on\ the outside.

Shoot. Could aliens read minds? Oh no. What if they found out what I had done? I was the one who fought the DM. What if they found out? Man oh man. This was bad.

Suddenly, a DM heliquad—a flying machine with four propellers, one on the top left corner, one on the top right corner, another on the bottom left corner, and the last on the bottom right corner—was hovering above the entire city, and everyone was horrified.

This wouldn't end well.

I did my best to scare the quad off but not hit it, which could cause it to fall and hit a building, injuring innocent people. The sun had just peeked over the horizon, so some of the sky was bright while other parts were dark.

All of the sudden, I saw Corbin in the heliquad, shouting my name. At first, I thought I was hallucinating, but it was real.

Everyone was in there was shouting at me to stop.

I did stop shooting lightning, but one lightning bolt had hit it earlier and caused so much damage that the blades stopped rotating. The heliquad shot toward the ground, picking up speed by the second. It was falling fast and heading straight toward a building. It landed on the structure, and all I saw were sparks and glass shattering.

I ran to the side of the building, which had a ladder extending to the top. I climbed and ran over to the heliquad to check if my friends were all right.

I asked what they were doing in a DM heliquad. They told me they had wiped out a Dark Multiverse warehouse.

Warehouse?

They said it was where they stored most of their war vehicles. That was when I noticed that two people were missing, along with Madison and Elijah. It turned out that Simon and Logan had taken a 2100 Crawler.

"They'll be here in two days," I was assured by Corbin.

"In a crawler?" I asked, surprised.

It was then that I realized my friends were a loose wreck without me leading our team.

Chapter 33

EZRA

Simon and Logan arrived two days later, and I made lots and lots of apologies. In the end, everything worked out, but I still felt like it wasn't enough to please myself and everyone else. About three days later, we heard there would be a big announcement in the center of Indimpoe. It looked like there was a big gathering. Mayor Tok was on a stage with a microphone.

"OK, I have gathered you all for an important announcement. The DDP, Danger Deduction Program, has now been installed!"

The crowd cheered. But then my head went dizzy, and I fell to the ground.

"Ezra?" I heard. I didn't know who said it, though.

My head spun, and everything went dark. In the darkness, I started to see a light. A light purple with a bit of orange mixed in. There was a shining clear object that looked like a diamond. That was the atmosphere amulet. Now, I understood! This was the temple. Then I saw Elijah and Madison strapped to a machine that was taking blue and red streaks out their head as the machine ran. I could hear screams and the sound of footsteps. Just then, Dr. Phoenix approached the machine. He turned a few knobs and the machine started making a loud buzz. More streaks were pulled out their heads, followed by more screams. Then I heard some wind and … birds chirping? Some pattering on the temple roof. It sounded like rain. Of course! The rainforest! Where else would the Phoenix Force hide captives than in a temple hidden in a rainforest? Just then, the vision started to fade, and I woke up again. By then the crowd had moved on, and it was getting dark. My friends, though, are shaking me wildly.

"Oh good." Matthew sighed with relief. "You're awake."

"I-I-I had a vision," I started to explain. "They're in a temple in the rainforest. That's where Dr. Phoenix is holding Madi, Elijah, and the atmosphere amulet."

My friends were surprised but listened to me.

"Yeah, we knew that, but which one?"

"Just follow me," I replied.

"Hey, stop right there!"

I spun around and saw three black SUVs parked by each other to make a wall. Then I saw six men with helmets and bulletproof vests. They also had things on their backs that looked like oxygen tanks. Their costumes were black, and their masks had a spot connecting their noses and mouths so they could breathe. There were three lines for the breathing part so the oxygen could get in and out. About where their cheeks were was where the masks came out about an inch and sloped and connected to the breathing part. They also had thick black blasters with red lasers pointing at us. On top of each of the blasters was a barrel full of swirling red-and-white smoke. I'd seen that before. It was what the investigators at our house had. It was one of those lasers that caught on fire.

"We are raid troopers, Phoenix's top fighters. Hands behind your heads and don't move!" one of them shouted. "Now!" Then one of the men pressed a button on his watch that opened a hologram of Dr. Phoenix.

"We've caught you," Dr. Phoenix spoke aloud. "And this time—" he chuckled "—this time, there is no escape."

The hologram ended, and the blue light was swarmed back into the trooper's watch. The men came over and put handcuffs on us. Corbin tried to escape the men, but he only got a few feet out when a raid trooper shot him with his laser. Corbin burst into flames. He threw a fireball at them but missed. Just then, Corbin froze. The fire went down, and he didn't move a muscle.

Standing behind him with his hand out was Vadg. The one man we trusted when we were in Zykele had just backstabbed us. It seemed like Vadg could freeze people like Medusa, just not to stone. He stuck his hand out again, and Corbin was back to normal. The guards took Corbin and slammed him against a vehicle while they put the handcuffs on.

They threw us into the back of the SUVs and drove off. I looked out the window and was stunned to see where we were going. The rainforest.

Chapter 34

ezra

The cars followed each other up a path through the town. When we got to the forest, we walked. We had been walking for about an hour when we saw the huge temple. We entered through the doors and saw Madi, and Elijah strapped to their chairs with the machine buzzing loudly.

"Guys!" I yelled.

"What's going on?" Elijah asked with an urgency in his voice.

They walked us up to the floor in front of Madi and Elijah. Suddenly, the floor opened up to reveal a pit of lava. Dr. Phoenix entered the room and pressed a button on the remote control that he had in his hand. It raised clear walls all around me and my friends, trapping us in a tiny room with a pit of lava below us. To make matters worse, the walls start closing in on us, resulting in us being pushed toward the lava.

"We thought we would do something original," Dr. Phoenix said. "So that's what we did!"

I glared at Vadg, who looked at me with a straight face. All of a sudden, I heard a quiet tap. Then another and another. Everyone went silent. A few pieces of rock fell from the ceiling. Just then, I saw the one thing that could make our death even more miserable. A monster broke through the ceiling and climbed throughout the temple. I had seen him before. He was the four-armed monster that Logan and his friends had fought in the war.

"No!" Simon screamed.

The monster jumped at Madison.

"*Ahh*!" she yelled.

The monster tipped over her chair and cut the rope. She stood up and cut Elijah's rope too.

"Freeze them!" Dr. Phoenix yelled to Vadg.

Vadg pointed his finger, but before he could pull something off, Elijah sprayed him with water. It wasn't much water because the machine had taken away most of their powers. They ran over to the glass.

"How do we get you guys out?" Madison asked.

Elijah looked at the machine that had stolen their powers. "I got an idea." He ran over to the machine. "With all these powers combined, we can crack the glass easily."

"Do it fast," I said. "The walls are pushing us into the pit."

Elijah messed with the machine, pressing buttons like crazy. Eventually a hole opened, and a thick laser shot and shattered the glass. My friends and I jumped, successfully made it to the other side, and ran into a hallway. As Dr. Phoenix turned to run, some of the rocks and plaster fell from the ceiling and blocked the small and hidden door. Rocks also blocked the path into the hallway we were in. The room would have been dark if it weren't for the torches that hung on the walls, but the hallway was pitch-black. We were stuck in a tight hallway with rocks blocking our exits.

"Ezra, are you sure that Phoenix can't break through the rock?" Elijah said. "I don't think it will hold them for long!"

Thump, thump—Phoenix banged on the rocks and tried to get through.

"They'll make it through any second now!" Corbin exclaimed.

We started to run down the hall, which was slowly starting to shift and crack.

"Guys, we need to hurry!"

The hallway was only a few feet across, but it was super long, so we didn't know where we were going. We just ran. Ran from Dr. Phoenix. Then we saw a soft blue light illuminate the hallway. What was this?

Chapter 35

EZRA

We neared the strange light. Soon we realized that it was the atmosphere amulet. We were running faster than lightning. Just then, Dr. Phoenix came pounding through and all the rocks began collapsing on top of us.

We reached the end of the hallway, but Dr. Phoenix was still chasing after us. The atmosphere amulet glowed blue and white. I reached my hand out, and the second my fingertips touched it, a small explosion knocked us backward, but Dr. Phoenix was still running toward us.

Where could we go? Just as Dr. Phoenix was about to blast us, the rocks from the ceiling fell. A huge rock pinned me down, but my friends were free.

"Look!" Simon yelled. "Go through the vent!" He pointed at a small hole, barely big enough for us to fit through. It wasn't a vent, just a little hole that had a pathway through it.

Madison blasted the rock off me. When she did that, the laser blasted a large hole in the wall. I was about to run through it, but rocks suddenly fell and blocked my path. Now it was just me and Dr. Phoenix. I made the only decision I could. I jumped through the odd-looking tunnel and army crawled my way through. The inside was plated with metal, and there were little holes about the size of pencil erasers on both sides of me. I wondered what they were for. I soon got my answer.

I knew Dr. Phoenix would try to stop me, but I never expected it to be this way. Smoke blew through the holes. Within seconds, the whole tunnel was filled with smoke. I tried to cover my mouth with my shirt, but it was no use. I choked and coughed and gasped for air. I tried to keep crawling, but I couldn't. My world went black. Was this the end?

I woke up. At first, I tried to open my eyes but couldn't. My ears worked fine, though. I heard ringing and then sirens blaring. I heard news reporters ranting about the newly discovered temple. I heard EMTs yelling and rushing nearby with equipment. I heard the forensic scientists wonder aloud about the scene. But most of all, I heard my friends yelling and snapping at one of the officers because they wanted to see my condition.

I wanted more than anything to tell them I was OK. But was I? Was I OK? Was I hurt but it hadn't kicked in yet? My eyes finally opened. I was on a stretcher being wheeled into an ambulance. I saw the temple in front of me. There were so many people doing so many different things. I couldn't see everything, though, because I was loaded into the ambulance.

Right before the EMT shut the door, Logan peeked through the crack and screamed, "Look! He's awake!"

A swarm of people crowded around the ambulance. A doctor ran to my stretcher and took my heart rate, temperature, blood pressure, and other medical stuff.

"Oh my!" she exclaimed. "His heart is basically skipping a beat, his temperature is 120 degrees, and his vitals are super low."

"Is he awake?" a man asked from the front.

"Yeah," she said, stunned. "Yeah, he's wide awake." She put her fingers on my neck to check my pulse again, but she jumped back and yelped. "His skin, it's … it's … burning hot!"

I felt my neck with my hand. It wasn't hot. It wasn't hot at all. What was she talking about? This had to be a dream. I closed my eyes and fell asleep.

I woke up in a large white room in a hospital bed. Corbin, Madi, and Elijah were all looking at me.

"Do you feel OK?" Elijah asked. "'Cause you don't look so good."

Madi elbowed him.

"Can I have a mirror?" I asked.

Madison hesitantly handed me one. She was right. I looked bad. My hair was dark black, and my face looked dark gray because of the smoke.

"Why was my skin burning?" I asked.

They all were quiet until Madison spoke up.

"Ezra, we have some bad news," she spoke calmly. "Corbin did some research. Millions of years ago, people like us, people with superpowers, were here on Earth. Some of them reported having burning skin and ended up …" She paused.

"And ended up what?" I asked.

"They ended up dying shortly after."

"How much is shortly?" I questioned.

"Two weeks to a month."

"Why?"

"It's your elemental core," Corbin said. "Your core is 50 percent built up of elements like fire, lightning, water, et cetera. So it usually doesn't have enough of the things you need to live to hold you up for your whole life like someone without superpowers has."

We were silent for the next minute or two.

"Where's the amulet?" I asked.

"Where it should be," Elijah replied. "With us."

Chapter 36

EZRa

We kept talking for two hours. Then the doctor came in. "Hello, Ezra. Nice to see you awake. Anyway, we have done some research as to why your skin is burning. We think we know why. When you were in that temple, your skin burned because of a lack of oxygen and hydrogen, or water, there."

That is useless information, I thought. "OK, so you're telling me that I need to drink or bathe in water? That is the dumbest diagnosis I have ever heard!" I shouted.

"OK, Ezra, if you are going to talk like that, then I will let you be," said the doctor. He walked out, and we started to talk more.

"Ezra, have you ever thought about why you are burning? I think it's because of the amulet. Since you grabbed the amulet, if that made you like this, it would make sense that if you get the opposite amulet, it will make you better," Corbin said.

"That is a good thought," I said. "But there is one problem with your plan. How do we get out of here?"

"I can't believe this," Matthew said. "You're saying Ezra could get better with the Earth amulet *and* nobody knows anything about the temple or the amulets?"

"Yes," I replied. "Nobody knows anything about it. They just think the temple was some ancient thing."

Just then, a rattling sound came from the hallway. The doctor slammed into the door and into the room. He held out one of the blasters that had white-and-red swirls in it.

"W-w-what is g-going on?" His voice was cracked and disordered.

I realized his body was glitching as if he were electronic. White lights flickered through him. He then was pushed by a gust of super strong wind, but only he could feel it. He stumbled back a few feet and then fell. He clutched the back of his head in pain. Then he reached out his hand and a hole appeared in the wall, overlooking the city below. A blue laser shot through the hole.

"Run!" I yelled.

We all scrambled behind something. More lasers shot through the hole. But soon, they stopped. Suddenly, a raid trooper flew inside. He wore a white suit this time with a white mask. His eyes glowed blue. He had another one of those blasters. (By the way, I guess they're called 9 Blasters.) But this time, the base was white, and instead of having white and red mixed for the energy, it was white and blue. He had a jetpack on his back and basically looked like a storm trooper. The glitching man had already glitched so much, he was barely there. Then he disappeared.

"Where's Simon?" I whispered. "We need him!"

The trooper, who worked for Dr. Phoenix, ran over and saw us crouching behind the desk.

"Get up!" he ordered. "Hands behind your heads."

We did as he ordered, and the trooper set his blaster down. Why was he doing that? Then he put his hands on his helmet and took it off. Smoke wafted out softly as his mask raised. I looked at his face and was stunned to see Simon smiling. Just before I could react, he shocked me with lightning. My eyes turned black as if they had shut down, and my body froze.

Part 4

AMULETS ARISING

Chapter 37

EZRa

When I finally woke up, I couldn't see anything. My eyes were open, but it seemed as if we were in a dark room. It was extremely difficult to see. I had absolutely no idea where I was. Everyone else was calm from what I could tell. They were crouching, but I had no idea why. That was when I noticed the glowing blue dart in my forearm. I didn't know what it was, but it seemed everyone else did. Then I attempted to hurt everyone who was with me.

It was sudden. They didn't seem surprised, though. I tried asked them what was happening to me, but when I spoke, this is what came out: "I am after ever*one of you."

So now I sounded and acted like a—hold on, I sounded like an evil alien. My voice was crackled and disordered. *So I'm an alien,* I thought. *I'm probably forever going to be hurting friends and family and innocent people who are driving or walking down the sidewalk.* Or maybe not forever.

All the sudden, something else was injected into my forearm.

So, I had in me what I thought was a liquid that would change me into an alien, and I had a liquid that I thought would change me back into a human. It was a mix of green, but some of it was transparent. And some of it was coming out my side. I had no idea what I looked like, except for the huge claws in place of my hands and needles in my forearms.

It seemed that I was inside a huge metal cage. I didn't even realize it because the room was so dark. The cage was very rusty, making it easy to break open. I just flicked my finger at it, and it broke into a thousand pieces on the ground.

Now all of my friends were running, and I was hot on their tails. Why was I doing this? I just couldn't control it. We ran outside into a busy street. As I was running, the ground cracked beneath me. It was probably many thousands of dollars' worth of damage for whomever owned this. There was an old abandoned taxi big enough for my friends and I to get in. Logan climbed in the driver's seat and hotwired the car to life. I hadn't known he could do that! I tried my hardest to catch up with them. Since I was so huge, I actually placed both of my feet in two separate cars, never to be driven again, and made my own roller skates. I heard yelling coming from behind me. It sounded like Bryce. He was yelling at me.

I spun around and roller-skated toward him. He was telling me to stop. That's when my monster thoughts came in.

"You're not gonna be livin' past today, kid. You can try to outrun me, but you'll never make it."

He just stood there, staring me in the eye. He threw something at me. I had no idea what it was. It looked as though it was going supersonic. Not that it hurt me, but it was a fast throw, and it would have hurt an ordinary human.

Chapter 38

EZRa

So there I was, standing there, doing nothing but giving death threats to Bryce, who seemed to still be throwing little rocks at me. I thought he was trying to reason with me and telling me to stop. To stop chasing them. My growling started, and he started talking more, about me stopping, stopping, stopping.

He meant not attacking anybody anymore. Not crushing stuff or trying to kill people. Just then, everything became a blur, and I couldn't really see faces clearly. The world shifted around, and just before I almost blacked out, I saw something. Something weird. Matthew jumped out of the car, his fist clenched. His hand almost glowed a blueish color, as if there was something in it. But as soon as he opened his hand, the sky went black and I couldn't see.

I heard my friends screaming in pain. It felt as if the wind had risen and everything around me was just ... floating. They stopped screaming, and the sky went back to normal. I saw pieces of the road, telephone poles, and all the buildings floating up in the air.

Everything was flying upward. Everything except me and the earth amulet, which lay on the ground, glowing bright blue and sparking with lightning around it. Grass was peeling up, and the Earth was breaking down. Worst of all, my friends weren't there.

At last, I blacked out. I woke up in a sweat. I shot up in the bed. Where was I? The sheets over me were white, but the room was dark. The door was cracked, and a dim orangish light burst through. I jumped out of bed and crept toward the door.

What I saw was definitely surprising. It was a rocket. Yes, a rocket, like NASA. It was in a room about as big as a football field, and it had the word, "PHOENIX" on it.

Just then, a hole in the wall opened up, and eight people walked in. Dr. Phoenix and Julian walked in, surrounded by his security guards in their white suits and carrying white 9 blasters.

Six moon buggies came rolling out onto a platform, which would then insert them into the rocket. Each moon buggy had blasters on it.

All of the sudden, I heard a voice say, "T-minus five hours until launch."

"Is the toxin loaded?" Dr. Phoenix asked.

"Loaded."

"Perfect."

Standing by Dr. Phoenix was a man who wore a black tuxedo and had slick black hair, a pale blue face, and glowing red eyes. Surely an alien.

"Are you sure that this will work?" the man asked.

"Yes, boss," Dr. Phoenix said.

Boss? I thought Phoenix was the leader.

"I don't want it to fail."

"Trust me, Banter, it won't."

"Hey," one of his security guards said. "Look over there."

Shoot. I forgot Phoenix security guards had thermal masks that let them detect body heat. The guard slowly crept toward the gray bucket I was hiding behind. Just as he peeked over the corner, I zapped him with a bolt of lightning. He fell toward the ground as everyone stared.

"Hey!" Julian screamed. "It's Ezra Woods!"

I launched up and bolted toward a barrier. The guards shot blue lasers at me, but I hid behind a Phoenix car. The Phoenix guards halted their blasting.

"He knows," Banter said. "We have to stop him."

"We're in a room full of machines," Dr. Phoenix said. "We can easily shut him down."

Dr. Phoenix walked into a machine, which was basically a full-size mech. The mech seemed as if it magically came to life. It was dark before, but when he powered it on, it started glowing orange. The mech started walking toward me. He picked up a car and threw it at me. I dodged it in the nick of time. The car collided with another, causing a large explosion. I shot lightning at one of the men, and the rest started shooting the neon blue lasers at me. I knocked out all of them until the only people left were Dr. Phoenix, Bunter, Colvin, and Julian.

"We need reinforcements," Dr. Phoenix said.

"It's four versus one."

The mech ran toward me as I shot lightning at it. No use. The lightning didn't affect the mech. He grabbed me by the neck and held me. Just then, the door blasted open. A large floating saucer full of people soared in. They started shooting at Dr. Phoenix's backup men, who had just arrived. Corbin jumped out as the rest of them kept shooting. Blue lasers shot everywhere.

"Thanks," I said.

"No problem."

Lasers continued to shoot back and forth. The mech tried to come toward us, but it was knocked down with a loud crackle. I looked over at the saucer. There were only five people left on the Phoenix Force security team. Corbin blasted four of them while Dr. Phoenix, Julian, and Banter ran behind the rocket. The one security guard left raised his hands, signaling surrender. He carefully took off his mask, and the face under it ... was Simon.

"Don't shoot," I said to my squad. "Let me take him."

"Ezra, don't," Corbin said.

"He left us. It's my duty to fight him."

Chapter 39

EZRA

Simon's suit looked advanced. It was all white like everyone else's, but his visor was glowing blue, which went well with his 9 blaster.

"Well, well, well," he said.

I was silent.

"You need to get a mind," he said. "You're never gonna beat one of the biggest armies in the world."

"Maybe not Phoenix, but I could take you out in my sleep."

"Yeah, right." He sneered. "Hey, maybe your lightning is more powerful than mine, but with all my gadgets, this will be like stealing candy from a baby."

He shot a rocket at me, but I dodged it. I shot up and shocked him with lightning. He bolted upright as the electricity sparked around him. He fell to the ground, and the grenade on his belt exploded.

"Ugh," he said. His face was pressed against the ground.

I walked over to him and stuck out my hand. He was quiet and still until he took my hand and pulled me to the ground.

"Hey!" I yelled.

He grabbed his 9 blaster and held it in front of my face. "I don't want to," he said, "but I will."

"Do it," Dr. Phoenix yelled.

"Yeah," I said. "Do it. I dare you."

He just stood there, thinking about everything.

"What? Are you too scared to take a dare from a former friend?"

"Get out of my head!" he yelled. Just then, he winced in pain and fell to his knees.

"What happened?" I asked.

I looked behind him and saw a man in a bulky red suit with a white glowing visor and a laser in his hand. He pressed a button on his wrist and flew away with his jetpack. I looked at Simon. He was gone.

When the red-suited man flew away, I turned around. Simon lay on the ground motionless while Phoenix's mech walked toward me. Just then, all the walls around me shot open and we were outside. The bright sun shone on my face. Now I could see the rocket clearly. There was a screen on the rocket that showed people sitting at a desk. I concluded that this was the control panel.

"Banter, Julian, get out of here. Let me take him."

My friends started shouting behind me.

"Don't lay a finger on him," Will yelled.

"Yeah. You even come close to hurting him, and you'll pay," Matthew said as lightning tubes sparked around his hands.

"Don't get into this," I said.

"T-minus four hours until launch," said someone through the screen.

"You have no idea what's going on," Dr. Phoenix said. "That rocket has a toxin in it, and when we launch the rocket, it will come crashing back to Earth and release the toxin for miles. There's no stopping it."

Chapter 40

EZRA

Phoenix's mech inched toward me. It was a big bright black suit with orange armor. It had "DM" painted on each arm and on the chest plate. The places that didn't have armor were glowing purple. I could see Phoenix standing by the control panel in the head of the mech. He swerved the joystick, and the mech's left hand flew into the air and balled its fist. He punched me, and I flew backward.

"I said don't touch him!" Matthew yelled. He jumped at the mech with a lightning hand.

"Don't!" Madi screamed.

Phoenix hit back, and Matthew slammed into the ground. I was blasted outside, and the sun was shining bright. It was really hot out, and there were buildings all around. Cars stopped in the middle of the road to stare at Dr. Phoenix's huge mech. The blaster on his hand shot another lightning ball at me. I somersaulted and dodged it while Phoenix prepared another blast. Just then, I saw my friends run from behind the mech and to my side. Logan and his friends weren't here. It was Elijah, Corbin, Will, Madi, and Matthew. Just like the beginning. Without Bryce.

"Guys, get out of here!" I yelled at them. "I don't want you getting hurt."

"No, we're staying here," Corbin said. "We're not leaving you."

Punch after punch. Swing after swing. We weren't winning our battle, but we weren't losing either. We fought while Colvin stayed hidden. The mech shot a bolt of lightning out of its hand that blasted against my chest and sent me flying backward. My back shattered a Starbucks wall. The workers inside screamed as coffee poured on me.

"Sorry! Sorry!" I apologized.

"What are you doing, young man?" a lady yelled.

What am I doing? I thought.

The burning coffee ran down my shirt. I ran out of the broken Starbucks and shot fire at Dr. Phoenix's mech, which stood right outside, waiting to humiliate me. The mech seemed to absorb the fire, but when it did, the suit started to glow a dark red and then went back to normal.

"I think it is absorbing our attacks, almost like a force field!" said Will.

"That's likely."

"Are you sure everyone else is away from here?" I asked.

"Yes," Madi said. "I just called Logan. He told me they're over on the other side of the city."

"Good."

Just then, Dr. Phoenix pressed a button on the mech, and it opened a blue swirl that sucked us in. We flew out on top of a building.

"Whoa!" I exclaimed.

Phoenix whipped at me with a punch that hit me in the ear. I fell down, and my head hung over the side of the building. Lightning flew out of the mech, and I flipped over and off the building entirely.

"Help!" I cried.

Just then, I saw a hand reach out for me. *I'm hallucinating*, I thought, but I reached out for it anyway. I felt a hand, but it felt like electricity. The second I touched it, four of my senses didn't work anymore. I couldn't see, hear, touch, or smell anything. The only thing I could feel was the wind rushing against my head until I couldn't even feel that anymore.

Chapter 41

EZRA

I still couldn't see anything, but I knew I wasn't in the air anymore. I felt a wall against my back and chains connecting my hands to the wall so I couldn't move them. I pulsed and electricity broke the chains. I was free. I walked around, still couldn't see, and searched for a door. I felt a doorknob, but it needed a key. I pulsed and the door blasted open. Outside the door was a small room, about the size of an elevator, with transparent walls. *No way,* I thought. I was inside the rocket! I saw the control panel below and the bottom of the rocket.

I looked left and saw Will and Elijah standing about twenty feet away from it. There were rocks on the ground. Dr. Phoenix stood in front of them with sparking hands. Will was about to shoot a blast of lightning, but he froze. I looked behind him and there was Vadg. Will collapsed to the ground, and Elijah looked around for help. Where were Madi and Corbin?

Just then I heard ... something. I crept into the dark room, which was now bright because of the sun shining through the door. I heard thumping. Repetitive thumping. It had to be the top floor of the rocket. I ran back into the small transparent room and saw Dr. Phoenix running toward the control panel. What had happened to Will and Elijah?

I had to do something, so I did something crazy. I took the metal chains and laid them on a large vent in the ground. I took ahold of the chains and pulsed. The vent shot open, and I could see the room below. It had to be like twenty-five feet under me. I jumped and smashed into the ground below hard, but I got up.

"Where is everyone?" I said to myself.

The room was full of debris. I was the only object in it that wasn't covered in dust. It was silent except for the sound coming from underneath the debris. I looked underneath and saw a TV. It was on and showed a plan for what the rocket was going to do. I didn't know what it was; it just looked like a blueprint of some sort. I thought I saw something about releasing toxins, but I wasn't sure.

All the sudden, a huge piece of debris came crashing down. I had to run before it could hit me. It came tumbling down onto the TV. *Great*, I thought. This rocket was different from a normal one. The tank of fuel was toward the bottom of the ship. I couldn't see it now, but I knew that on the very last level, half of the fuel container was inside the rocket and the other half was outside. I ran to a window and looked outside. I could see the mech there, but I couldn't see Dr. Phoenix. There were also a couple of policemen but not any of my friends.

I ran around the room and saw exactly what I needed. An elevator. I ran inside and pressed the "1" button. The elevator was very fast. I got to the control panel within a matter of seconds. The door opened, and as far as I could tell, nobody else was in there. You could see half of the huge container that held the fuel. I ran up to a TV screen and saw two kids standing in a tight room. It was them! I pressed a button that said "microphone" on it.

"Guys, it's me."

Just then, the rocket turned on with an ear-piercing screech. I looked onto the screen.

"Ez**ra!**Help!" I heard Corbin yell.

"Madi! Corbin! Where are you guys?" I yelled.

"We're**n the ro*ket*at the*******."

"Hey!" I heard behind me.

I spun around. Colvin Phoenix was standing there.

"Well, well, well, Colvin Phoenix," I said confidently. "After all this time, you finally gathered up the neutrons of your courage and came to me. Face-to-face."

"At least I'm not one of you," Colvin said. "We have something. We're this close to ruling the world."

"Nobody's gonna like you," I said in defense. "Why don't you join us?"

"I'd like to help you out," Colvin said with an evil grin. "Which way did you come in?"

I sighed. "This is useless," I said.

Just then, he punched me in the mouth. I shocked him back with lightning.

"Come on. Just tell me where my friends are at least!" I said.

"Fine. They're in the top level. It's a little room. Just go through the elevator."

I smiled. "Thanks."

The elevator was fast. The door opened.

"Corbin! Madi!" I said. "We have to get out of here!"

Just then, a countdown of sixty seconds started. The rocket ship was about to blast off! We ran to the elevator and went back down to the control room. We saw Colvin and Dr. Phoenix talking.

"We have to go!" Dr. Phoenix said. "Ezra Woods is onboard."

"But Dad—"

"We have to leave," Dr. Phoenix said sternly.

They left the rocket, but I saw Dr. Phoenix turn a corner and twist a knob. Liquid poured out of the tank. That was the fuel!

"They took out the fuel!" I exclaimed. "We're so dead!"

Colvin and Dr. Phoenix ran outside. Colvin watched the countdown.

"I can't do this!" he finally said. "I'm going in!"

Colvin ran back onto the ship.

"Colvin!" Dr. Phoenix yelled.

The countdown only had fifteen seconds left.

"Let me help you!" I smiled.

Corbin, Madi, and I went down the elevator to the main floor.

"Help us control the rocket!" Colvin started pressing buttons on the control panel.

The countdown was down to five seconds.

"It's no use!" I said. "The ship is gonna go off without any fuel!"

"This isn't good," Corbin said. "We're gonna go to space, but without fuel, we're going to crash right back to the ground. The explosion could stretch for miles!"

"Even worse," Colvin began. "My dad put a toxin in the rocket. When it crashes back down to Earth, the toxin will release. It could kill millions."

"What toxin is it?" Corbin asked.

"*Um* ... it says here that it is called hyloden. Made up of acid and burning gas. It is the second most toxic element in the multiverse."

"OK. Good news and bad news," Corbin said.

"What's the bad news?" I asked.

"Bad news is I can't figure out how to stop the rocket."

"And the good news?" Colvin asked.

"The good news is the toxin isn't the number one."

Chapter 42

EZRA

"How many feet are we at?" I asked Colvin.

"Just got to two thousand," he replied. "I don't think we can stop it. We're running out of fuel, and this is gonna crash back down to Earth."

"Unless ..." Madi said. "We land it in the ocean."

"Great idea," I said. "How long is it from Puerto Rico to like ... Portugal? We could land it in the Atlantic Ocean. We just need to know how far that is from here."

"Already on it," Colvin said and typed it on his computer. "3,775," he replied.

"How far does the toxin release?" I asked.

"*Um ... uh-oh,*" he said softly.

"What?" I asked.

"It was so close," he began. "But it's 3,777 miles."

"OK," I said. "I can fix that." I looked at my phone. "Colvin, keep driving the rocket."

"Aye, aye, captain."

I pulled up my calls and called Kyler.

"Hey Ky, we need you to get everyone out of the area of the rocket for about two miles."

"How are we supposed to do that?" Kyler demanded.

"Tell them there's a hurricane coming within two miles."

"OK. I'll show someone," Kyler said.

"Thanks."

We hung up, and I ran back to the control panel. I hadn't realized it, but Colvin wasn't there. There was only a note.

> The rocket is going to crash into the ocean. I've put it to the exact point so it will land where we want it to. The middle of the Atlantic Ocean. Corbin, Madison, and I have jumped out, but the only place you can jump out from is on the top floor. There are boats waiting for us. You need to jump out too.

"This is great!" I exclaimed. But I spoke too soon.

Just then, a flashing red alarm went off, and a TV fell from the wall and onto the steering joystick. The steering joystick broke off and fell to the ground, and the rocket jerked in a different direction.

"Oh no."

Now the rocket was aiming toward somewhere completely different than where it was supposed to go, and we couldn't change it because the steering wheel had broken off.

"What are we going to do?" I heard from behind me.

I spun around, and Colvin was standing there.

"Colvin!" I exclaimed. "You were supposed to jump out!"

"There weren't enough parachutes," he replied.

"OK. I know how we can fix this," I said. "You need to make a dome made of force fields outside the ship so that when the toxin escapes, it can't get out of the dome."

Just then, the rocket stopped in midair and started sinking, picking up speed by the second.

"And right as the rocket crashes and the toxin releases, you jump out," I concluded.

"And what happens to you?" he said.

"Well …" I said. "I don't live past today."

"No. Then I need to drive the ship and you jump out."

"I'm not doing that," I replied.

"You're not going down."

"Yes, I am."

"Then I'll go down with you."

We were both silent.

"Fine. I can't make you change your mind," I said. "But you make the force field dome."

And he did it just in time. The rocket crashed into the water, and it filled up fast. The force field stood strong. Our heads were barely above the water.

"Thank you for helping me," I said.

"Anytime," he replied.

And then we were completely submerged.

The End

Stay tuned for …
The Multiverse 2: Fall of Immortals

About the Authors

Jonathan Fetzner-Roell
Jonathan Fetzner-Roell is an eleven-year-old author who loves writing about action, adventure, sci-fi, and drama. He attends St. Malachy Parish School and enjoys writing with his friends. In addition to writing, Jonathan enjoys playing basketball and soccer. He has plans for many other book series as he grows as an author.

Connor Harrity
Connor Harrity is an eleven-year-old author and friend who enjoys writing chapters of thought rather than action. He attends St. Malachy Parish School and enjoys writing with his friends. He has played piano for six years and wants to pursue a career of music. His favorite song is "Piano Man' by Elton John.

Hunter Hopf
Hunter Hopf is an eleven-year-old boy who loves to create dark and scary chapters. He is the inventor of the book's shadow. He loves to help with the technology aspect. He too attends St. Malachy Parish School.

Alan Navas-Brito
Alan Navas-Brito is eleven years old and attends St. Malachy Parish School. In addition to writing Alan enjoys hanging out with his friends. He enjoys writing stories about magic and fantasy.

Printed in the United States
by Baker & Taylor Publisher Services